fine

Sweet

Published by Sweet Cherry Publishing Limited
Unit 36, Vulcan House,
Vulcan Road,
Leicester, LE5 3EF
United Kingdom

First published in the UK in 2019
2019 edition

2 4 6 8 10 9 7 5 3 1

ISBN: 978-1-78226-480-4

© Gill Stewart

Galloway Girls: Lily's Just Fine

Cover design by Rhiannon Izard

www.sweetcherrypublishing.com

To David, Alexander and Zachary,
you are all very fine.

Lily

Gemma says, 'So how come *you* get to go to the prom?'

We're sitting on the bench that overlooks the harbour, eating ice cream. The waterfront is one of Newton St Cuthbert's claims to touristy fame, but it's too early in the season for visitors. It's warm, though, so we've taken off our Galloway Academy blazers. I've pulled up my skirt and unbuttoned most of my shirt. We're on the south coast, even if it is the south coast of Scotland. You can always hope for a tan.

'Why shouldn't I go?'

'Because you're only sixteen? And you're not in the sixth form?'

'So? I got them the venue. I arranged the decor. In fact, I've organised the whole thing. Oh, and I'm going out with the head boy.' I interrupt a complacent smile to lick some ice cream dripping down my cone. 'Aargh, that was close!' Chocolate ice cream on a white school shirt – not a good look.

Gemma is still going on about the prom. 'Yes, yes, I know all that. But why is it always you? You shouldn't even be on the organising committee.'

'I'm not on it officially; it's just that they couldn't manage without me.' I know I sound smug, but hey, why not when you've got a lot to be smug about? 'They were the ones who came and asked me, when their first venue fell through.'

'I bet they didn't expect you to take over the running of the whole thing.'

'I haven't taken over. Well, not completely.'

Gemma sniggers and nearly has an ice cream catastrophe of her own.

I say, 'Hey, do you want to come too? I can maybe find you a partner. I'll talk to Gerry Hawkins, or Dan, or–'

'No, no,' she says hastily. 'I didn't say I wanted to go. I'd have to get dressed up and all that stuff.' She shudders. 'I just don't understand how you manage to get involved in everything.'

'I told you, it's because I *do* things.' I've tried to explain this before. Gemma just sits back and lets things happen. I don't understand how people can be like that. You should take life by the scruff of the neck. Get things done. Otherwise, what's the point?

I'm actually quite looking forward to the prom (stupid American name, but that's what the sixth form voted to call it). The school has never used the Abbey House Hotel before, with its fancy ballroom and views over the river. The lilac colour scheme was my idea and it's working out brilliantly. I'd even considered wearing a purple dress, but decided that would be a bit too much – and I definitely do not want to blend in with the trimmings! Instead I've gone for a silky sheath in aquamarine, with a slit right up to my knickers. I don't think Mum's too keen on it, but she's always suggesting I wear something other than jeans. My clothes are pretty much the only thing about me she seems to take an interest in these days. Fortunately my sister, Corinne, backed me up, so I got my way.

'I suppose I'd better go and start getting ready.' I lick the last of the ice cream from my fingers. 'Want to come and be my style adviser?'

Gemma shakes her head. 'I do not. I'm going home to watch daytime TV, eat rubbish and *not* study. The bliss.'

She's just taken her last exam. I finished a couple of days ago, but I can still feel the relief. 'Bliss,' I echo. No more revising. Summer coming. Life is good!

We head back into town. I don't have far to go. My parents' house is in one of the pretty, pastel-coloured Georgian terraces the tourists are always oohing and aahing about, right near the town centre. Gemma lives in a semi in one of the newer estates farther out. She moans constantly about the walk, but when I suggest she get a bike she just ignores me. Come to think of it, she ignores me quite a lot.

As we reach the corner where our routes part she says, 'Will you keep an eye out for Tom? He's going to the prom too. He's definitely not looking forward to it.'

'Tom Owen?' I'm slightly put out. There aren't many people in our year going, and I certainly wouldn't have expected Gemma's quiet neighbour to be one of them. 'Who's he going with?'

'I'm not sure. One of Sonya Robson's crowd. Morag? Yes, I think it's Morag. She wanted him to wear a kilt but he's refused.'

'He'll have to wear a suit, at the very least.' The organising committee have been very strict about the dress code – with just a little nudge from me.

'Yes, he knows. He's probably dreading that too. I thought you could just say hi to him, so he doesn't, you know, feel like a total outsider.'

'Okay, no problem.' I haven't got anything against Tom Owen – he's just one of those people who fades into the background. But I like to help when I can. And I almost always can.

Tom

I'm cooking chicken fajitas. It's something Sarah will usually eat, even if she only manages half of one, and Mum loves them. Plus they'll keep if Dad doesn't get home in time for dinner. Not that I'll be eating with them tonight – you get food at the stupid dance.

Sarah's having a good day. She's been up in her dressing gown since lunchtime, and now she comes through to the kitchen to talk to me while I cook.

She sits on one of the stools at the breakfast bar, all pale and drooping, like it's been an effort to get up there.

'You shouldn't be cooking,' she says. 'You should be getting ready to go out.'

'Getting ready's not going to take long: put on horrible suit, finished.'

'You should at least have a shower first.'

I shrug. 'I had a shower this morning. Look, I'm not trying to impress anybody.'

'But still. Your first prom …' Sarah sounds wistful,

grey-green eyes dreamy behind her thick glasses. 'Will you take photos?'

I let out a snort before I remember how much she would love to be the one going – or at least to look forward to going in future. But she's been ill for years. As far as I can see, the chances of her ever attending a prom are just about nil. 'I'll do my best,' I say instead, trying to sound more enthusiastic, 'and I'll tell you all about it tomorrow.'

'Thanks.' She flashes me a smile, something hardly anyone outside the family sees, even those who do bother to come visit. 'Listen, pass me the peppers and I'll chop them. That'll help speed things up, won't it?'

I remember not to say *Are you sure?* or *Don't do too much.* I hand over the chopping board and the shiny red peppers. I even give her the onion to do, to show I have faith in her. It isn't much help, she's so slow, but I don't tell her that.

When Mum comes home she makes even more fuss than Sarah about me going to get ready. It's easier just to give in. They're all excited about seeing me in a suit and tie, and don't I look grown up, and does Morag know how lucky she is to have me as her partner? As if. I know for a fact I'm at least her third choice. That's why I said yes. I didn't want her to have to go on and on asking people, plus I hadn't had time to think up a good excuse.

Whatever. I agreed to go and now I just have to get on with it.

Lily

Dressing up is fun! I've put my hair into these big curlers so it's come out all bouncy, and I've shaved and moisturised, highlighted and contoured until I feel like a whole new me. I wish Corinne was home to help, but I do my best and go to show Mum the results.

She's in the conservatory with the doors open to the garden. The early evening sun lights up the garden and it looks beautiful, the lilac bushes in bloom against the old stone wall, and all sorts of other flowers starting to come out. 'Ta-da!' I say, twirling to get her attention.

For a moment she doesn't react. Then she looks up from her magazine and smiles faintly. 'Very nice, darling.' After another pause she frowns, again faintly. 'Maybe that split is a little too revealing?'

'It's nothing. I am wearing pants, you know.' I wonder if she'd even notice if I was showing a bit of side bum. Probably not. I say brightly, 'And the neckline is very demure.'

Mum sighs. Okay, maybe "demure" isn't the right word. But the neckline is definitely high – no flesh on display, although the shimmery material certainly shows my boobs off to good advantage.

'Is Jamie walking you there?' Wow, Mum is really making an effort to be interested.

'Walking! It's nearly a mile. I'd never manage that in these heels.' They're three inches high, which makes me over six feet. Jamie won't be happy that I'm the same height as him. Hah! 'He's borrowing his mum's car. Should be here to pick me up any minute.'

'He won't be drinking, will he?' Mum sighs again, like it's all too much for her.

I say diplomatically, 'He's only seventeen, they won't serve him at the hotel.' Knowing Jamie he'll find some way to get hold of some alcohol and we'll end up getting a taxi back, but there's no need to tell Mum that.

Just then my phone goes off and it's Jamie saying he can't find a space and can I come outside. Parking on my street is ridiculous, so there's no real reason for me to feel miffed that he hasn't come to the door.

I say goodbye to Mum and grab the tiny glittery bag Corinne picked out to go with the dress before hurrying out. There's already a car hooting at Jamie from behind, so I jump in and we head straight off.

He's wearing the full kilt outfit, including a black jacket, but not (thank goodness) one of those laced-up shirts.

'Looking good,' I say as we head through the town.

'And you,' he answers, without looking.

Things are crazy when we get to the Abbey House Hotel: parents dropping off their kids, taxis queuing, a few new drivers with borrowed cars like Jamie trying to park without embarrassing themselves. Everyone else is milling about outside, waiting for the photographer to take a picture of us on the broad steps. They've stuck to the dress code – even Debby-Lou in a long Gothic dress, long black hair and long black eyelashes. The boys are adjusting tight collars and trying to hide cans of beer. The girls are squealing and kissing cheeks, as though they haven't just seen each other a couple of hours ago.

'You look gorgeous, babe.'

'Gorgeous yourself!'

'Sonya's missing a bit of her dress, ha ha!'

'Nothing that matters! Not sure about the dye job, though.'

'It's not nearly as bad as Debby-Lou's.'

'No, that looks totally fake. Sonya's looks more like Lily's.'

Gee, thanks. I thought my curls were pretty stylish, not to mention the colour is natural.

The photographer takes an age, then finally everyone starts to head inside. Jamie stands at the door of the reception room, telling people where to go.

'There are seating plans,' I mutter. 'I know because I drew them up.'

'I'm just trying to be helpful.'

'Point them in the way of the seating plan, then.' As far as I can see, the only thing he's doing is blocking the entrance.

He smiles brightly at everyone but me. 'You're being bossy again.'

I'm being bossy? He's the one personally telling everyone where to go.

'Come on, Rob's already over there.' I take his hand and pull him to our table. He doesn't look happy, but at least it allows everyone else to get into the room. He releases my hand as soon as he can and turns to talk to his friend. I really hope he isn't going to sulk.

Lily

The evening isn't as good as I'd expected. Most of the boys have done too much pre-drinking – and some of the girls, too. Sonya is waaay out of it. Everything I can control is absolutely fine: music, dress, food, even the behaviour, up to a point. But actually the whole thing just isn't that ... *exciting*. Most people seem keener on taking stupid selfies than chatting or dancing.

I collect a soda water from the bar and go to hang out at the back of the room, to try and work out what I can do to improve things. Tom Owen is standing there, which makes me remember my promise to Gemma.

'Hi,' I say, waving my glass. Oops, nearly spilt it. 'How's it going?'

He's a thin boy with a narrow face, not quite as tall as me in these heels. I've always found him to be a bit of a loner. Certainly he's never the centre of a crowd like Jamie. Recently he's let his dark blonde hair grow out and the way it hangs in his face makes his expression hard to read.

'Oh. Hi.' He glances at me for a moment and then away.

'Who are you here with?' I say, trying to remember.

'Morag Leslie. And you?'

That's a bit much. Everyone knows I'm with Jamie – even if I haven't actually been *with* Jamie much this evening. He seems to think it's his duty to dance with practically every girl in his year, not to mention some of the teachers who've come along to supervise. He's really hot on keeping in with the teachers, is Jamie.

'Oh yes, Jamie,' he says, and it's almost like he's sneering.

That makes me turn and look at him properly. I want to point out that he has *nothing* to sneer about. But he's tossed his hair back and I'm distracted by his totally stunning eyes: sapphire blue with dark bits in them, like dark pools of summer sea, focussed on me with a questioning look.

For a moment I lose my train of thought.

'Huh?'

'Where is he?' Tom repeats, turning that gaze from me to the crowd beneath the strobe lights.

'How should I know?'

'I thought you knew everything that's going on.'

He says it so deadpan that I can't tell if he's trying to be sarcastic or not. Either way, before I've worked out a reply, he's disappeared out of a side door with his phone to his ear.

Well. That was pleasant – *not*. That must be the first time I've had a one-to-one conversation with Tom Owen in years, if ever. He's Gemma's friend, not mine. I'd thought he was kind of sweet because he was always quiet and well behaved. Now I'm not so sure.

Jamie insists on us being the last people to leave, like we're the hosts or something. A bit ridiculous, but I don't object to extending the evening. I'm still waiting for something thrilling to happen. For it to live up to my expectations.

We say goodbye to Mrs Broadfoot, who's the last of the teachers to go. She's head of Pupil Support so she apparently feels responsible for us all. Plus, I think she has a teeny crush on Jamie, who does look pretty good in his kilt.

Finally we get into Jamie's mum's car. He doesn't start the engine so I turn to him, wondering if he's going to move in for a kiss. Suddenly I don't really feel in the mood. I'm pissed off with him for ignoring me all evening.

Instead he says, 'Lily, I think we should talk.'

Uh-oh. That's never the start of something good.

'Talk away,' I say brightly, scooting around further so I can see him properly. It's handy that there are lots of lights in the hotel car park.

His expression is serious, which makes him

more good-looking than ever: short, neat hair, slim, symmetrical face. Sometimes he can look the tiniest bit bland. Now he looks grim and interesting.

He's looking towards me but not really at me, certainly not meeting my eyes. 'Look, you know I'm off on this school trip to Nicaragua next week, then after that to France with the parents, and then I'm off to uni.'

'Ye-es.' Of course I know all that. We've discussed it already and I'm fine with it. It's not like I'm the clingy type. I function perfectly well on my own.

'Well,' he says, and pauses.

Jesus, why doesn't he just get on with it? I know what's coming now.

He says, 'Maybe it's time for us to take a break, meet other people, you know? I wouldn't want you to feel I was away having a good time and you were left here ...'

'I wouldn't feel that, believe me,' I snap. What is he on? Does he think I'm going to be languishing in my room? 'I'm quite capable of having a good time whether you're here or not. But that's fine, we can go our separate ways.'

He lets out a sigh of relief so strong it ruffles his light-brown fringe, and the grim expression goes back to bland. What did he expect? That I'd make a scene? Burst into tears?

He says, 'I'm glad you're taking it so well,' and then just sits there, like he's not quite sure what should happen next.

'It's fine,' I say again, although I could have done with him being a little less relieved to be shot of me. 'Right, shall we go home then?'

'What? Oh, yes, if you're sure.'

Maybe the last girlfriend he broke up with made a scene. Actually, as that girlfriend was Sonya Robson, she probably made a *big* scene. Now he's realised he's going to get away with this so easily, he hurries to start the car. The roads are quiet and it's only a few minutes before we reach my house. He's driving faster than he usually does, like he's desperate to get away from me.

I slide out of the car before he's decided whether he needs to give me a goodbye kiss or not.

I raise a hand in a vague farewell. 'Thanks for the lift.' I almost add *Have a nice life!* but decide that would sound like I care.

He drives off and I'm left with my fury. How dare he finish with me? I'm the one who makes decisions like that. *And how dare he be relieved?*

But the really annoying thing is that I'm a bit relieved, too. Maybe he's made a decision that I hadn't yet realised needed making. How mind-blowingly infuriating is that? Now everyone will think I care, and I don't.

I really don't.

Tom

Gemma says, 'Did you hear Jamie broke up with Lily?'

She doesn't wait for my answer, which would have been 'No'. I'm not interested in that kind of stuff, but it looks like I'm going to hear all about it anyway.

Apparently it happened at the dance last night, presumably later on. They'd certainly arrived together, Jamie looking all smooth and self-important, Lily just looking like, well, herself, and turning every head. I don't know what it is with that girl. She isn't pretty, but she has something about her that makes people want to look. Not me, obviously, but a lot of people.

Gemma's still going on, ' ... and he said it was because he was going to be away so much and it wouldn't be fair on Lily. But he must have wanted to break up, really, mustn't he? If he was keen on her like he used to be, he wouldn't even have signed up for the Nicaragua trip.'

'Looks good on his CV,' I say automatically. Wasn't that why everyone signed up?

And thinking about it, I'm not sure Jamie has ever been *that* keen on Lily. More keen on the kudos of being seen with her, on what a striking couple they made. That must have been before he realised the downside of spending so long in her company. Not that I know Lily Hildebrand well, but I've observed her from a distance and heard more than enough about her from Gemma. She's been Gemma's best friend forever, but even Gem has to admit she's *hard work*. Like she always has to be right, and she has all these ideas and so much energy.

Which immediately makes me think of Sarah, who's paying for the effort she made yesterday helping prepare dinner, and now has no energy at all. Life is so unfair.

'I can't decide whether Lils is upset but too proud to show it, or genuinely not upset. Which would mean that she didn't like Jamie that much after all, despite them going out for six months, which is the longest she's ever been out with anyone.'

Does it matter? I want to say, but apparently it does to Gemma.

We're sitting on the broken-down summer seat in Gemma's back garden. She insists on having the sunshade up because the sun only needs to glance at her skin to burn it. And as soon as she burns she worries about skin cancer. There's one thing you can say for sure about Gemma – she knows how to worry.

'How's Sarah?' she says, changing the subject abruptly as though she's realised I'm bored.

'She's not so good today.' I keep my tone neutral.

'I gathered. Your mum said she didn't want to see me.'

'It's not that she wouldn't want to see you, it's just …'

'She's tired.'

'Yes.' I let out the tiniest of sighs. How can a fifteen year old girl be this tired? And how is it they can't find out what's wrong with her? She's been like this for over two years now. At first they'd talked about post-viral fatigue. Now they say maybe it's Chronic Fatigue Syndrome, but they don't really know. They've done tests for every illness I've ever heard of (and lots I haven't) and found nothing definite.

'There're lots of pictures of the prom online. I thought she'd like to go through them with me. I could tell her who everyone is, fill her in on the gossip.'

'She'd love that.' And it would be a lot more fun for Sarah – and for me – if she looked through the photos with Gemma. 'Maybe she'll feel better this afternoon.'

'Okay, message me if she does and I'll come over. Now I'm going to go home and finish my book.' Gemma pulls back her fine, reddish hair, squinting out into the sunshine. 'And I need to think of something to do to distract Lily. She's only happy when she's active. I don't suppose you have any ideas?'

I shake my head, alarmed to even be asked. I might feel very slightly sorry for Lily Hildebrand having been dumped by her perfect boyfriend, but I doubt it will make much of a dent in her immense self-confidence and otherwise wonderful life. I'm certainly not going to waste time dwelling on it.

Lily

It doesn't take long to realise that I've taken my eye off the ball. I'd known Jamie was going away for the summer, and I certainly hadn't counted on him keeping me entertained if he wasn't. But stupidly, I haven't made any plans of my own.

I need to decide how to make use of all this time – ten whole weeks of it, stretching out like a great blank space before me. Three of those weeks are for wrapping up the school term, but who does any work at this stage of the year?

I get up early, upload some pictures, and talk to Gemma who seems desperate to know All About It. Then I take Mum a cup of tea, because that way I know she's awake. I think about bullying her to get out of bed but don't have the energy. She asks how the prom was and I say fine. She doesn't mention Jamie, so I don't need to tell her anything there.

I find a sun lounger and carry it into the garden,

setting it up on the decking at the far end where you get the most sun. Then I lie down and think.

Finally I'm going to be able to do all the things I haven't had time for. I'd had loads of ideas, I'm sure I had. But now I can't think of a single one of them. And something's been niggling at me. It's the tone of Gemma's voice, all full of sympathy. Yes, she'd been curious, too, but I can handle that. I'm used to people being interested in my life. But *concern for my wellbeing*? No way. I don't need anyone to feel sorry for me. I'll be fine, just like always.

Jamie Abernethy – smart, sporty, good-looking Jamie Abernethy – had broken up with me. So what? There are other fish in the sea if I want one (a boyfriend, not a fish), and as it happens, I don't right now. I'm perfectly okay on my own. I just have to make sure everyone knows that. I'll go on as normal but more so, and no one will *dare* feel sorry for me.

Right. So how am I going to do this? Be normal but also *new* and *interesting*?

I don't like to diss the town where I was born and brought up, but it's hard to think of something new and interesting to do in Newton St Cuthbert – or Galloway, even. Maybe I should go and stay with Corinne in Edinburgh like she's always asking me to.

No! I am not going to do that. That would look like running away. I'm going to find something to do right here.

Okay, so start with the easy things: get fit – that's been on the agenda forever, why not make it happen now? Dad'll be good for a new pair of trainers, maybe some fitness gear. I can have a whole new image: Lily in Lycra. And maybe I should pay a bit more attention to my diet? Not to lose weight, but I could definitely eat more healthily. I'll do more cooking!

I grin to myself. I'm cheering up already. That's two things decided, although cooking's not that visible. Which is fine, I don't just do things because they're visible, but right now it's important that I'm not thought to be moping. I do *not* mope.

Surprisingly, it's Gemma who provides the best idea of all. Something fun and useful – and very public indeed.

She comes round in the late afternoon to cross-question me/offer more sympathy. I cut her short.

'Didn't expect to see you out walking in the sunshine when you didn't absolutely need to be.'

'I thought you might appreciate some moral support.'

'I don't,' I say. Sometimes you have to be blunt to get the message across. 'What's that?' I indicate the flyer she has in her hand.

'It's, er,' she looks more closely. 'I'm not sure. Someone stuck it in my hand as I was walking through town. Something about the gala.'

She hands it to me so I can read it myself.

'Gala committee,' I read aloud. 'Newton St Cuthbert's annual gala takes place in the first week of

August and we need new blood! Young or old, long-time resident or new, it's you we're looking for!'

'Oh god,' says Gemma. 'Now I remember. It was Mrs Hebden who gave it to me. That's why I didn't dare put it straight in the next bin. You weren't in her Biology class. She's always going on about how the gala committee need more input and how we shouldn't leave everything to the same old people.'

'She's right. You shouldn't.' I tap the paper thoughtfully. 'You know, this might be a very good idea. This could be fun.'

'Are you mad? You've just finished on the prom committee. Even you can't possibly want to get involved in something like this.'

'Yes I can.' It's exactly what I need – and Gemma too, although she doesn't realise it yet. 'We'll have to get our thinking caps on. Gala Week has been the same forever. They're right, they definitely need new blood.'

Gemma is looking anxious. 'It'll be too late to change things for this year. They'll have most of it arranged already.'

'And who says arrangements can't be altered?'

'They're not really looking for people to have ideas,' she says, looking panicky now. 'They're adults. You won't be able to boss them around. I bet they're just looking for gofers.'

'They might *think* they're looking for gofers. That isn't necessarily what they're going to get.' I feel happier than I have done all day. 'They're having an open meeting on Monday evening. We have to go.'

Gemma opens her mouth in horror, revealing small, neat teeth. 'Wha-at? I'm not going. You know I hate that kind of thing.'

'All the more reason to do it.' I grin. This is going to be amazing. We are really going to make a difference. Then I tone down my expression and use my trump card: 'And it'll be so good for me to have something to distract me from, you know ...'

She falls for my sad face and plea for support way more easily than when I just straight out tell her what to do. I'll have to remember that.

Tom

It's Sunday afternoon and John Forsyth, the commodore, has asked me to go down to the sailing club. It's my least favourite time – too bloody busy – but he wants me to help out coaching some of the kids. It's only fair: people gave up their time to coach me and Sarah when we were younger. Dad's down there as well, manning the rescue boat, but Mum stays at home. She says she needs to catch up on the washing and ironing, but it's really so that Sarah isn't left alone.

Sarah used to love going down to the club. She was way more competitive than me, had the makings of a really good sailor. Now she rarely leaves the house.

I feel bad going down there without her, being able to enjoy it when she can't. Maybe I can try to work something out. Get Mum to drive her down on one of her good days, even if she just sits on the jetty, hears the wind in the rigging, smells the raw, salty, seaweed smell. That should do her good, shouldn't it?

Or will it just make her regret all she's missing even more? She'd been very quiet after Gemma went through the prom photos with her last night, kind of withdrawn. I wish I knew what she was thinking.

I wish I could make her better.

But I can't, so I take my frustration out on the squealing eight- and nine-year-olds, telling them to concentrate or that boom is going to come round and hit them … Ah, there it goes. A bash on the head may be what they need, it tends to quieten them down.

In the late afternoon, when most people have gone home because the wind is dying down, I take Dad's ancient Mirror out to the Flett Islands. It's a biggish boat to manage on your own, but it handles better than the Toppers the kids were using, and something about the touch of the varnished wood, the smell of the faded sail, makes me feel good about life.

There's more wind out at sea (we kept the kids in the estuary) and suddenly I have that feeling; the one you get when the jib and mainsail are taut and the water is hissing beneath the keel, splashing up salty and sharp in your face.

You have to concentrate on what you're doing and you can't think about anything else. You *are* the boat, the wind, the water. It's bloody fantastic and I want to go farther, out towards the Isle of Man and on and on. But I don't, of course. I tack when I reach the southernmost island – little more than a clump of rocks and grass – and head back to shore.

Like every sane person who's just finished their Higher exams, I've been planning on an easy few weeks running down to the end of term. Okay, we're back at school for now, but no one takes it seriously at this stage.

Then Gemma comes up to me at lunchtime on Monday. She practically sidles up, and she has that anxious look on her pale face so I know she wants something – that and the fact that we don't really hang out together at school. We're neighbours and she's good with Sarah, but we're in different crowds. Well, she's in Lily Hildebrand's crowd and I'm mostly on my own, which is the way I like it.

'Hiya,' she says, sitting down on the bench next to me where I'm finishing my lunch.

'Hiya.' I take a last bite of my apple and put the core inside the Tupperware box.

'You doing anything this evening?'

'Maybe.' I haven't got anything planned. Mum did a huge vegetarian chilli last night and there's plenty left over so I don't need to cook, but I'm not going to lay myself open to some invite I don't want to accept. Look what happened with Morag Leslie. Just thinking about that suit makes me put a hand up to my neck to loosen my tie.

'The gala committee are looking for volunteers. There's a meeting at seven.'

'I know.' I was in Mrs Hebden's Biology class too. I'd heard *all* about it.

'Lily and I are going along. She – we – thought it would be good if a few other young people came too, you know?'

She looks at me beseechingly. I know who's put her up to this. For whatever reason, Lily Hildebrand has decided that people should go to the meeting. And what Lily decides, happens. I can see her right now at the edge of the playing fields, tackling a group in the year below us, hands flying, head nodding, bulldozing over what I imagine are objections.

The gala committee? Not my kind of thing.

'Please say you'll come,' says Gemma. 'I'll get my brother to give us a lift back in so you won't have to walk.'

As if that's the reason I'd say no.

'It'll be fun,' she says, her eyes wide and desperate. 'I don't want it to be just Lily and me.'

And like with Morag Leslie – like an *idiot* – I find myself saying, 'Okay then, why not?'

Lily

We get three other teenagers to come along to the gala meeting. That's a pretty poor turnout, but Gemma seems amazed we persuaded anyone. She talked Tom Owen into it (they seem to get on well together – I wonder if there's anything going on there?), and I nobbled Alice Beaumont and Kelly Smith from the year below us. They both have parents who like them to Get Involved so it wasn't too difficult. I still have hopes of drawing in more people when they see what fun we're having, but five is a start.

We wait for Alice and Kelly on the pavement outside the Town Hall. I don't want them to be nervous about going inside on their own. That's just the kind of excuse they'd give for not turning up.

They appear just when I've got my phone out to give them an earful. They're not even hurrying, and I can hear the tail end of their conversation as they arrive. Alice is saying, 'Aye, that's right, Jamie Abernethy ...'

and they both look at me like they've been talking about me.

I glare and hustle them into the meeting room. Mrs Hebden looks totally stunned when we walk in. The meeting is in a side room of the Town Hall and there are only enough seats for ten people. That'll need to change.

She says, 'You've come for the gala committee?'

Well, obviously. Why else would we be here?

'We saw your flyer,' I say, ushering the others forward when they seem inclined to head right back out. 'Sounded like it might be fun.' I give her my best smile and she returns it cautiously. I try again, 'You said you were looking for volunteers?'

A grey-haired man at the head of the table says, 'Yes. Er, excellent. Come in. Find yourselves a seat.'

'I told you this was a bad idea,' mutters Gemma as we get chairs from the stack by the wall.

Fortunately, it doesn't take Mrs Hebden long to decide that our presence is a good thing and all down to her. She introduces us to the other committee members, who are all so old they make her look young. The man at the head of the table is the chairman. He's got a bristling grey moustache and a look of self-satisfaction. He nods to me when he hears my name, so I'm guessing he knows Dad from somewhere. Probably the golf club. He looks that type.

They go through the meeting agenda, discussing all the things they've already organised. Gemma was right, they aren't looking for any input from us. They clearly think it's too late to introduce any new ideas.

They're wrong.

'There's not much in there for teenagers,' I say, waving my hand vaguely before speaking but still receiving a glare from the chairman whose name seems to be Simon.

'There's the fancy dress competition,' says Mrs Hebden.

'For the under-10s,' I say.

'And the Scottish country dancing display,' says Simon.

I just manage to stop myself groaning out loud.

'And the crowning of the Gala Queen, and the procession.'

'We still have a Gala Queen?' I'm completely stunned. That shows how much interest I've taken in Gala Week recently. Basically none since I grew too old to enter the fancy dress competition. 'That is so last century. Totally sexist. I can't believe–'

'The Gala Queen is an excellent way of getting young people involved,' says Mrs Hebden loudly. 'Until you five showed an interest, she was the only youngster on the committee. It's a pity she can't be here until later, but she's having her first fitting for the dress.'

'Who on earth is it?' I ask, still shaking my head at this appalling state of affairs.

'Sally-Anne McKay,' says Alice, looking at me as if

I'm the weird one. 'She's in our year. It was announced in assembly and everything.'

The name brings to mind a slim, pretty girl with long blonde hair. No offence, but she's just the type the committee would pick.

I open my mouth to protest some more but the man Simon says, 'The issue isn't up for discussion. If you wanted to have any input you should have joined the committee sooner.'

'But–'

'We still need to discuss street decorations,' says Mrs Hebden loudly. 'Perhaps we can move on to see if anyone has thoughts?'

I decide to leave it for now but I haven't given up. Newton St Cuthbert is our town too. I am not prepared to be associated with a gala that has something as backwards as a Gala Queen as its centrepiece. The beginning of an idea for how we could change things occurs to me and I ponder on it, wondering how I can get it to work.

The adults start getting all excited about bunting, which is apparently what you call those little flag strings they put up each year. Are they too tatty to use one last time? Is everyone happy with the colour scheme? I keep quiet. I can do that when it's something I don't care about either way.

Pretty, smiley Sally-Anne McKay appears in the middle of that discussion, full of apologies for being late. The adults all beam at her in a really sickening way. She's totally their favourite kind of teenager: quiet, obliging, never rocks the boat.

And then I have another brainwave that doesn't take any pondering at all. Newton St Cuthbert's a harbour town, isn't it? The place is renowned for its sailing. Shouldn't the gala include something to do with boats?

'A mini regatta!' I say, or maybe I shout. 'That's what you need. That'll be something different.'

Mrs Hebden frowns at me. 'I don't know ...'

'You should raise it under Any Other Business,' says another woman. 'You shouldn't shout out like that.'

I wave my hand to Simon. 'Sorry. Can we put that down under AOB?' It's such a brilliant idea I decide I can be patient and fit in with their fuddy-duddy ways.

For once an adult seems to be on my side. Old Simon says, 'A regatta? Well, well, well. Yes, young lady, you might be on to something there. We'll get to that in a minute. Yes, you know, I think that might well work.' He rubs his hands together and looks so pleased you'd think he came up with the idea himself.

Tom

As soon as Lily Hildebrand says the word "regatta" I want to get up and leave. Most of the adults look bemused while she expounds on it. I've noticed people tend to do that a lot when Lily's around. But the chairman strokes his moustache and nods, and Lily is already turning to me.

'You sail, don't you Tom? You could take that on.' She says it like she's doing me a favour.

'I do a bit of sailing.'

'You teach the little kids, I remember Gemma saying so. Hey, why don't we do more than just a regatta? We could do a whole series of lessons in the lead-up, involve lots of new kids in learning to sail. Then in Gala Week we could have special races for them; plus proper races for the experienced sailors. It'll be great!'

I shake my head. There are too many reasons why this is a bad idea for me to even start listing them, but number one is that it'll be a hell of a lot of work.

The old guy who's chairing the meeting says, 'That's rather interesting, young lady. I really don't know why the sailing club don't do their own regatta, but as they don't, why not incorporate it into our festivities?'

'Didn't they used to do one?' Mrs Hebden is frowning like she's trying to remember.

I know why it stopped. Because no one except John Forsyth did a bloody thing to help and when he had that heart attack his wife said enough was enough.

I say, 'It'll take a lot of organising.'

Lily comes back in that infuriating way of hers. 'So? I'll help. So will Gemma. We've nothing else to do.'

'I've got lots to do,' says Gemma quickly, although I'm pretty sure it's a lie. She was moaning on the way here about how bored she's going to be over the summer. 'And anyway I don't know the first thing about sailing.'

'Nor do I,' says Lily happily. 'But I love learning new things! That's the whole point. And most of the organising will be nothing to do with being in a boat. Even if you're dead set against being in a boat, Gem, you can still help out.'

'Well, well, we're certainly getting some interesting ideas here,' says the chairman, beaming around. Sadly he's got over his initial reservations about Lily.

Mrs Hebden looks like she wants to put her head in her hands. Serves her right. If she didn't want us here, she shouldn't have given out those stupid flyers.

Not that I'm on Lily Hildebrand's side.

As soon as the heavy double doors of the Town Hall swing shut behind us, I turn to her.

'This is *not* a good idea.'

She looks at me all innocent. 'What isn't?'

'The sailing regatta!' I don't often shout but now I'm seriously pissed off.

Lily raises her eyebrows. 'Calm down, you're scaring the children.' She gestures to Sally-Anne, Alice and Kelly who titter as though she's said something clever.

I wait for them to walk on and then hiss at her, 'Listen, I haven't got the time.'

'That's crap. What else have you got to do? Exams are over, holidays nearly started. Hey, you're not going away in the holidays are you?'

I wish I could lie and say yes, but she'd find out soon enough. Besides, doesn't everyone know we *never* go away? 'No, I'm not. But I'll still be busy. There's a lot to do at home.'

'Ah.'

The way she says it, I know Gemma's been talking to her about Sarah. I really don't need Lily Hildebrand's sympathy. Sarah's illness is private. So I find myself saying, 'Okay, okay, I might be able to find time to help you. But I'm not doing the whole thing myself. Someone'll need to convince John Forsyth to get involved, and he won't be pleased he hasn't been consulted. And you and Gemma are going to have to learn to sail.' That'll show her.

'Not me,' says Gemma. She's kept out of the conversation so far, but this must be too much for her.

To my surprise, Lily nods. Her dark hair falls over her face and has to be tossed back. She puts an arm around Gemma and gives her a hug. 'It's okay Gem, you can do other stuff to help.'

That's when I remember Gemma has this thing about water. I was an idiot not to think of it sooner and I feel bad because she's biting her lip and looking unhappy.

I say, 'Aye, that's fine Gem, you don't have to do anything you don't want to do.'

Lily nods approvingly. 'So Gem can help with on-land organising, Tom will be in charge of the sailing, and I'll – I'll help out where necessary.'

Gemma and I look at each other. This isn't going the way we want at all.

Lily ploughs on. 'I really wouldn't mind learning to sail. Especially if you think it's necessary.' She grins at me. 'So how about you give me a couple of lessons? When you've got time, of course.'

I really should have known better than to make that suggestion. Instructing Lily Hildebrand in anything would be a challenge, but I really can't see her being at home on a boat. She's so big. Tall and not fat, but … *large*. The word "voluptuous" springs to mind.

I sigh. I want to back out but can't see any way of doing it now without losing face.

'Okay, fine,' I say and try not to notice her smile growing even broader because she's getting her way yet again.

There is one good thing that'll come out of this: Sarah will be pleased. She hero-worships Lily from afar so she'll love that I'm apparently going to get to know her better.

I shake my head. How did I get into this?

Lily

When I get home after the committee meeting it's nine thirty. I'm wide awake. Mum has already gone to bed. She seems to go up earlier and earlier. I'm sure she didn't use to sleep so much. It's annoying because it would have been nice to tell her about the meeting. Sometimes it's hard to find anything to talk to Mum about, but this would have been perfect. And if she's in bed I can't even put on any music. Never mind. I get a pen and pad out instead. I'll make a list! Once I had that idea about the regatta, all sorts of things started popping into my head. I didn't want to scare the committee too much by suggesting them all there and then. I'll write them down and drop them into the conversation one or two at a time. This year's gala is going to be the best ever!

We definitely need some more competitions. They have the fancy dress one, but they have that every year. What they need is something new. Something messy and fun. Kids love that. Could we do something with clay? Modelling? Or maybe that would be too difficult ... We might need a kiln. A design-your-own T-shirt competition? Has that been done before?

My gaze drifts out of the window, across the darkening garden to the walls painted pale blue to match the house. Beyond them the river is an inky smear along more orderly gardens, the neighbour's topiary a slightly sinister smudge.

I force myself back to my notes, which despite the heading "Best Gala Ever" are in danger of being overrun by doodles.

I cock my head. Doodles.

Doodles, graffiti ... graffiti, wall ... wall, paint ...

I swear, sometimes I amaze even myself.

What if the competition could be *more* than just fun? What if it could be useful too? The local play park has been an absolute eyesore since graffiti bandits decided to "express their creativity" all over the concrete wall. A bunch of kids could certainly do better. We could give it to them as an art project, divide it up into individual sections. Or have a theme. Get them to work together on a mural. It doesn't even have to be a competition, it could be all about teamwork. Community.

I make a few notes with more than a few exclamation marks, then sit back with a satisfied sigh.

Okay, so what about the teenagers – the group the committee has so conspicuously ignored? Unless you count having a Gala Queen, which I definitely don't.

And it isn't *just* about the sexism, either. This whole thing has reminded me of Corinne.

My sister had been a shoe-in for Queen when I was only seven or eight. I'd been so excited about it. Then, at the last minute – and despite her being 'anointed' confidentially beforehand – they chose someone else. It wasn't until years later that I understood why: that Corinne had been secretly seeing the niece of one of the committee members. When they all found out, she'd suddenly become persona *extremely* non grata.

Just thinking about it makes me royally *pissed*. And in that mood, I forget about competitions and start to expand on the idea that occurred to me during the meeting. What we need is a new parade, one that includes everyone.

I check online to see what's out there, and make *lots* of notes. After I've finished with the parade, I jot down a few other possibilities. Some kind of singing competition? Or something to do with cycling? Lots of money has been put into the cycle paths around town; maybe we can promote those as something other than a quiet place for underage drinking. I'll let the committee discuss it. It's important they feel like they're the ones making the decisions.

When I've finished my lists (for now) I look up the website for the local sailing club. The regatta idea is brilliant, if I do say so myself. It's something all ages can be involved in. We're a seaside town, we're known for sailing, so what was more obvious than this? And we have someone on the committee who's ideally placed to set it all up. Tom Owen doesn't realise it yet, but he's going to be invaluable.

I don't know why I've never done any sailing before, but we're going to rectify that. I wonder what Tom will be like as an instructor. It's a good thing he isn't as soft as I used to think. He'll be far more use to me, as a coach and as a fellow committee member, if he can stand up for himself.

Tom

I'm telling Sarah all about the stupid gala committee meeting and how Lily pushed me into getting so involved. It's almost worth the hassle to see Sarah's smile.

'Wow, that is so cool. Lily's like a force of nature, isn't she?'

I don't know why she says that like it's a good thing. 'I'd be happier if I was teaching her and Gemma both to sail at the same time, then Lily might not be quite so overpowering.'

'But Gemma's scared of water.'

'Gemma's scared of everything.'

'No she's isn't. She just worries.'

'Yeah – about everything.'

Sarah mutters something under her breath, which might be, 'I know how she feels.'

I don't know what to say to that. I want to tell her she doesn't need to worry – that she shouldn't worry because that really isn't going to help her. But nobody ever stopped worrying because someone told them to. Plus I have this worry of my own. That maybe Sarah's whole illness is psychosomatic, *caused* by too much worry. I definitely can't say that.

'Gemma can swim, can't she?' Couldn't everyone? Weren't we forced to learn in primary school?

'She can, just about. But she hates it. Don't you remember how she wasn't even keen on the big paddling pool we had a couple of years ago?'

I remember, fleetingly, how much fun we'd had. How Sarah had been wild and silly, and Gemma wary.

Sarah returns to the subject that interests her most. 'Are you really going to teach Lily Hildebrand to sail?' She sounds wistful – envious, even.

'Unless she backs out.' Hopefully she will. *I'm* certainly not going to. I'm okay as an instructor, she'll be horrendous as a pupil, but so what? I'm not going to be the one who wimps out.

'Good,' says Sarah. Then she looks at the stairs in that hopeless way which has become so familiar, as though to climb them is more difficult than climbing the Merrick with bare feet.

I stand up. 'You going up to bed? I need to get a book. Let's go up together.'

'If you want.' She shrugs as though she's doing me a favour, and pushes herself slowly to her feet.

I move to her side and put my arm round her

shoulders, all big-brotherly. That way we can pretend we're joint partners and I'm not helping her at all.

It would have been fine if Dad hadn't come home just then. He's been working late as usual.

'Sarah! Are you okay? Is Tom helping you upstairs?'

My sister sags against me, as though she really can't be bothered pretending anymore.

'We're fine,' I say, but he's already rushed up beside us, putting an arm around Sarah in a way that makes it clear he's strong and she's helpless.

'Off you go,' he says to me. 'I can manage from here.'

Sarah says nothing, which makes it even worse. When she's having a good day, at least she argues back.

Tom

Lily Hildebrand lives in one of the poshest houses in the town. I don't know what her father does but he must be making a mint. The house is in the old part, but it doesn't open directly on to the pavement like most of the others. Oh no, Lily Hildebrand's house has its own paved courtyard at the front, surrounded by fancy wrought-iron railings. And at the back, of course, it looks directly on to the river.

Living somewhere like that, it's really strange she's never done any sailing.

I call for her bright and early on Saturday morning. It's a good time to be out in the estuary, the tide is just right, but mostly I've chosen it because I'm sure she won't be happy to have her lazy Saturday morning disrupted. Gemma wouldn't have been, and even Sarah, when she still had energy and enthusiasm, loved a weekend lie-in.

But Lily appears at the door before I've even pressed

the fancy, antique-style bell. She looks annoyingly perky.

'I'm ready! I didn't want you to ring the bell, my mother's still asleep. Let's go.'

She's dressed in Lycra shorts and trainers. She'd have been better off with wet shoes like me, but trainers will be fine for now. With a fleece and a windcheater zipped up for extra warmth, there's nothing I can really criticise. The shorts are a bit revealing, but her jacket covers most of them. You can't deny there's an awful lot of Lily – lots of hair, lots of smooth white skin, lots and *lots* of curves – and it makes me a bit uncomfortable being up close to her.

'I'm still not convinced this is a good idea,' I say as we turn down the narrow path beside her house, heading for the water.

She looks innocent. 'What isn't?'

'This sailing regatta thing. There's a lot to organise, and hardly any time.'

'Which means the sooner we start the better. I phoned John Forsyth. He's the commodore, right? He says he'll be down here about ten, so we can talk to him after you've given me a lesson.' She grins, all pleased with herself. Lily Hildebrand is pleased with herself a lot.

'I knew he'd be around this morning. He always is.' I'm not going to let her pretend she's arranged everything.

'Well, I didn't know. Actually, I think Simon Archer must already have spoken to him about the regatta, he's keen to talk over the details with us.'

I'm even more annoyed. I don't want to do this bloody regatta, but if I am going to be involved I don't want everyone else meddling. If Simon Archer has upset Forsyth, it'll be a really crap start.

'We'll take out one of the Toppers,' I say, not prepared to go into any of that discussion with her. Toppers are small, but ideal for beginners. 'This one will do. You lift the tarpaulin off and I'll go and collect a couple of buoyancy aids.'

One of the many annoying things about Lily Hildebrand is that she's pretty capable. She listens to what I say, doesn't seem nervous about the water or the way the boat sways about, nods at my explanations and only asks the occasional question to make sure she's understood.

Initially I make her sit right towards the bow (there's not much room in a Topper), while I sail single-handed, explaining what I'm doing. Then we swap places and she has a try herself.

'You know this is actually fun!' She beams at me, dark eyes bright and laughing, hair tucked up inside a ridiculous pink cap.

'It is. Why have you never learnt before?'

She frowns. She has a very expressive face, all the features a little too big, too pronounced. She's odd-looking, but in an interesting way. 'I don't know.

Corrine – that's my sister, she tried it and didn't like it. And I was into other stuff like drama.'

'But with the sailing club on your doorstep, you would have thought …'

'I think Mum wasn't that keen. It was easier for her, less worrying, if we did things on dry land.'

'And your dad?'

'Oh, Dad's never here.' She says the words breezily, but there's a hint of something else in her voice. Regret? Resentment?

I wonder about that. My dad works in the local council. He's manager of some department and puts in long hours, but at least he's home every night. He's still part of the family, still involved in everything we do. In fact it was him who got Sarah and me into sailing, one of his great enthusiasms. I almost feel sorry for Lily Hildebrand and her absentee father. Until she tacks just when I'd told her to wait, and the boat tips so wildly I nearly slip right off the bow. 'Watch it!' I grab the mast just in time. 'Jesus.'

'Soooorry,' she says, but she doesn't sound apologetic. She might even have been laughing. 'I keep forgetting which way to move the tiller.'

'Time we headed back in.' I straighten myself and prepare to explain again about the tiller and rudder. A lot of people struggle with that to begin with.

She doesn't listen. She's already looking at the shore. 'Look, is that John Forsyth? Let's hurry up. It's nearly ten and I don't want him to think we're unreliable.'

'He knows I'm reliable,' I say, but she doesn't seem to hear. I show her which way to move the tiller and make sure I'm holding tight this time. The sluggish little boat makes its way, almost directly, back to the jetty.

Lily

Gemma wants to know how the sailing lesson went. She's even walked into town before lunchtime just to find out.

'It was fine. Easier than I thought.'

She pulls a face. I wonder if there's anything we can do about her water phobia. I've tried before a couple of times, but she completely vetoes any of my suggestions. It hasn't seemed that important, but now, with the regatta planned and after having so much fun on the boat, I think it might be time to give it another go.

'And did you speak to the commodore person?'

'Yup. It was easy. He'd been desperate to reintroduce some kind of sailing event for a while, but his wife was stopping him. Now he's got our support he's all for it. I'm going to suggest to Simon Archer that we set up a regatta subcommittee and John can be on that, along with Tom, me and you.'

'You don't need me,' she says quickly, chewing the end of a tail of hair.

'Yes, I really do,' I say. 'Tom Owen is still being less than enthusiastic, although I'm sure he realises deep down what a good idea it is. You know him better than I do. I need you to help me manage him. Pleeease, Gem?'

She looks worried. 'You can't "manage" Tom. He's quiet, but he can be pretty stubborn.'

'But you know him best. He'll do things for you.'

'Not necessarily,' she protests, but she doesn't say anything else about not being on the subcommittee so I've won that argument.

'Have you heard anything from Jamie?' she asks. So she's still worrying away at that, even though I've told her twenty times I'm over him.

'Not a thing,' I say cheerfully. 'And now that last year's sixth form have all left school, I don't see him at all. Not that I'm bothered either way.'

'He'll be getting ready for the Nicaragua trip.'

'Probably.' I can't even remember when they're leaving, that's how interested I am. 'Listen, I've got some more ideas for events during Gala Week. Tell me what you think ...'

Gemma is moderately positive about my plans. More so than Simon Archer at the next committee meeting. He's impressed with the amount we (well, mostly I) have arranged already, but he isn't too keen on the T-shirt design competition, or the wall-painting idea. 'It all sounds rather messy,' he says, stroking his silly moustache. 'You'll need to get permission to do anything with a wall in a public place. It'll take a lot of organising, and finding people to supervise.'

Mrs Hebden nods. 'You have no idea how much is involved in this kind of thing.'

Oh, give me strength. Haven't I just organised the prom practically single-handedly?

I say, 'Gemma and I'll do some of it. Alice is doing Higher Art so she's the ideal person to help.' Alice looks appalled, but doesn't actually refuse. It's always best to make suggestions like that in public. 'I'll have a word with someone in the Art Department at school, see how they organised painting the bike sheds. I might have to speak to the council, too.'

'I suppose you could make enquiries.' At least Simon hasn't disagreed out of hand.

'The Saturday is already going to be very busy,' says Mrs Hebden.

I nod eagerly. 'That's why we should run the wall painting Monday to Friday. We'll need the whole week so we can have different groups on different days, and the paint can dry overnight. Alice and I will come back to you with more details.'

Alice shakes her head but I'm on a roll.

'And I had another idea.' I ignore the increasingly worried expressions around the table. 'How about some kind of talent contest? Or an open mic session? Or even – radical thought – *both*! You know, "The

Newton St Cuthbert Talent Show". That kind of thing. It would get people involved as competitors and even more people would come along to watch.'

Mrs Hebden narrows her eyes at me. 'Lily, we've already got a draft of the programme drawn up for printing. It won't be possible to change it now. I only just managed to add the regatta in as a stop press.'

I wave that aside as the minor issue it is. 'We can always do an extra flyer; a kind of subprogramme for young people. It'll make it clear these events are a bit different, not the run-of-the-mill gala stuff.'

'The traditional elements of the gala are very popular,' says Mrs Hebden, looking offended.

'And introducing some new ideas will make it even better. We'll draw up a flyer and you can see what you think.' There, I can be as open and collaborative as anyone else. 'I'll write the list of what should be on it, and Alice can do the artwork.'

I think I hear a snort of laughter and look down the table to my left. I'm pretty sure it came from Tom Owen, although his face is perfectly straight by the time I meet his eye.

'I've never done anything like that before,' says Alice.

'All the more reason to try now. You can add it to your art portfolio. Think how good that will look.'

'I suppose ...'

'There's someone else who might be interested in working on it with you, if you wanted.' Gosh, Tom

Owen, making a suggestion off his own bat? He is coming on.

I nod encouragingly. I keep forgetting I'm not actually chairing the meeting.

'My sister Sarah does art. She might be willing to help.'

'That's a brilliant idea,' says Gemma. 'Sarah's really good and it would be great for her to be involved.'

Mrs Hebden nods, too. She must know the situation.

'I thought she was ill,' says Alice, looking confused. 'She's never at school, is she?'

'She's getting better,' says Tom firmly, and a little abruptly. 'She's doing her design course online.'

'Oh, okay. I didn't mean ...' Alice looks at her friend and they both shrug.

Tom turns to me, 'If you emailed stuff or gave it to me to take home, Sarah could work on it there and then email you back.'

'So, that's another thing sorted,' I say, smiling at the chairman so he knows to move on.

It's only when the meeting has finished that I realise I forgot to share my big idea about the parade. Oh well, I'll work on it some more and have a fully fledged plan next time.

Tom

Lily Hildebrand is unbelievably bossy, but to give her credit she does get things done. Look how she's even got me being all pro-active and volunteering Sarah's help.

I make sure Gemma and I get away quickly once the meeting's finished, just in case Lily ropes me into something else. We walk home through the quiet streets. Gemma seems in a good mood, and even comes in with me to tell Sarah what's been happening.

Mum's watching the news but she's always happy to see Gemma. She tells us to go on up to Sarah's room; she's still awake.

Sarah has the room that used to be mine, at the front of the house with a view over the town towards the river. It's the bigger of our two rooms. It makes more sense for her to have it than me, as she's home so much more of the time. We made the swap last autumn, when she obviously wasn't going to get back to school for a while. I don't really mind, although there's less privacy in the room at the back, right next to Mum and Dad.

She's wearing pyjamas and a dressing gown – I need to remember to try and persuade her to get dressed tomorrow – but she's sitting on top of the bedcovers which I know is a step better than being in bed. She grins when we come in.

'Hello there. How did it go? Was it fun?'

'It was a committee meeting,' says Gemma, plopping down on the end of the bed, 'therefore not fun.'

'But did you decide on stuff? Was Lily there?'

That's what Sarah really wants to know. Lily is the girl Sarah imagines she could be, if she wasn't ill: active and mouthy, super-confident. But Sarah would never be like that. She's quiet, like me.

'Lily was there and her usual overbearing self.'

Gemma looks at me reproachfully. 'Lily puts in a lot of hard work.'

'Because she wants to.'

'Well, yes. But the result is the same.'

I don't bother trying to explain that if you're working hard because you like doing it, you shouldn't get nearly as many brownie points as if you're doing it but not enjoying yourself (like me).

I turn to Sarah and say, 'We've found a job for you, if you want to do it.'

Her eyes widen and she hooks her hair nervously behind one ear. 'Me?'

'We want to pick your brain,' says Gemma, being extra-cheery to counter the nervousness. 'We need to create a leaflet to hand out for the gala. I think Lily called it a flyer. Anyway, Tom had this brilliant idea that you could help.'

'I don't know … What would I have to do?'

'Just look at the artwork, make some suggestions, maybe do the layout.'

Sarah moves her head slightly from side to side, which she always does when she's doubtful. 'I might be able to do that. Maybe.'

'Of course you can,' says Gemma. 'Lily will be really pleased. This is for the events aimed at younger people. If you can make something that will appeal to them, that'd be great.'

'I'll try,' says Sarah.

I can see she likes the idea of Lily being pleased, and it's great seeing her take an interest. I just hope it won't tire her out. If she can do most of the design on her laptop, it won't be too different from her usual messing around. Maybe this is the way forward, giving her the chance to push herself. At least I hope it is.

Lily

On Tuesday morning Mum is actually up before I leave for school. She makes herself a cup of black coffee and sits at the kitchen table with me. After a long silence she seems to realise that maybe she should be saying something. Unfortunately what she comes up with is, 'Are you and Jamie still seeing each other?'

Well, that certainly came out of the blue. I didn't think she'd noticed.

'No, we split up a couple of weeks ago. Didn't I tell you?'

'I'm sorry, Lily. That's a shame.'

'It's fine. I'm fine.' Jamie and I had some good times together, but I'm now convinced I'm much better off without him. And the gala is benefitting too. If it hadn't been for Jamie breaking up with me, I might never have joined the committee. But I don't say any of that to Mum. I hunt for another topic. She's stirring her coffee round and round, watching it swirl. She hasn't yet had a sip. 'You should eat some breakfast,' I say.

She looks up at me, she's so surprised. Normally she doesn't interfere with me and I don't interfere with her. Sometimes I check if she's awake, make her a drink. That's it. I'm busy enough with other stuff.

'I will,' she answers. 'Later.'

I know from the vacant look in her eyes, and the dull tone, that she won't. She seems to have no interest in food anymore. In anything, really. She cooks if Dad's home, but that's less and less often. And I had that idea that I was going to do more cooking, go on a health kick, but I haven't managed it yet.

I go and put on a slice of toast, buttering it when it's ready. That's the way she likes it – just buttered. I cut it in half. 'Here. Have this.'

She looks at it blankly. She seems tired, though god knows how she can be, all she does is sleep. 'Thanks,' she says. After a moment she picks up a piece and takes one small bite.

There. I've done my bit. I feel like I should do more, but I don't know what. I do know this isn't how family life should be. Surely it didn't use to be like this? We were never a model family like Gemma's, with her mum and dad always around, but things had been okay. These days Dad seems to spend more time in the London flat than here – when he's not in New York or Tokyo or god knows where.

I say, 'I'd better go now. I don't want to be late for school, do I?'

She doesn't answer. It was a rhetorical question anyway. It's only a five minute walk to school – three if I'm running late. This morning I actually have plenty of time, so I saunter along the street of houses painted pink and blue and cream, noting who's done their window boxes, and what flowers they've put in. I definitely prefer the ones with geraniums, bold and red.

But even as I think all of this, I'm chewing over what happened at breakfast. I've been ignoring it for a long time, but now I get a kind of sick feeling in my stomach as I admit to myself that there might actually be something wrong with my mum. She's never been exactly lively and outgoing, but now she's so slow she's practically comatose. And she's *way* too thin. She always used to be slim, but even Dad must notice she's now verging on gaunt. I wonder when he'll be home again.

If he isn't back in the next few days, maybe I'll phone Corinne and talk to her. Or Jonathan, my older, more remote brother. He's a doctor. Surely he'll know what's wrong. Yes, that's a plan. It's good to have a plan.

Nevertheless, a slither of unease stays with me all day.

Tom

At lunchtime on Wednesday I track down Lily Hildebrand to tell her Sarah wants to be involved with the flyers. She called out as I was leaving for school, asking if I really thought she'd be good enough. That means she's keen, and I don't want her to miss out.

Lily is alone for once, sitting on the red sandstone wall near the main school entrance, peeling an orange.

'It's good she's interested,' she says, although she sounds a bit preoccupied.

'Aye, it is. I don't think Alice was very enthusiastic, but as you've already asked her maybe you should let her give it a try.'

'I'll email the list of events to her and your sister, see who gets on with it first. I can't be bothered with slackers. If Alice doesn't get her finger out, too bad for her.' That's more the tone I expect from Lily Hildebrand: hectoring and aggressive, not distracted.

'I'll give you Sarah's email address,' I say, looking

in my bag for something to write on. 'Actually, I don't think I know hers, so I'll give you mine and then forward the stuff to her.'

She puts the orange aside, wipes her fingers on her school trousers, and takes out her phone. It's one of those oversized things, practically a tablet. Trust her to have something top of the range. 'I'll put it straight in here. When you find your sister's email address, can you send that to me too?'

She types in the details and then picks up her fruit again. She hands me a segment of orange. 'Have some. This is my second one.'

I take it, although I'm not sure why. It's not like I usually chat with Lily. I normally don't have anything to chat to her about.

I lean awkwardly against the wall. It would be rude to walk off straight away.

After a moment she says, 'You looking forward to starting Sixth Year? What subjects are you taking?' She seems happy to watch the groups of kids passing to and fro; happy to chat.

'Advanced higher maths, physics and chemistry.' I say it quickly. They're pretty dull choices. Sarah says I'm crazy to be doing all the sciences. 'You?'

'Advanced higher drama, same in media studies. Plus intermediate hospitality, just for something to fill up the timetable a bit.'

'I quite fancied doing hospitality. It's supposed to be fun.'

'I hope so.' She grins and kicks her heels against the stone wall, clearly much more at ease than I am. 'I'm planning to really get into cooking this year.'

'Cooking's okay,' I say, thinking how boring it is when you have to do it even when you don't feel like it. I usually cook on the days Mum has to stay for meetings at work, or when she takes Sarah for her appointments. Sometimes it's a real pain.

I hook my bag over my shoulder, ready to move on, but Lily is still talking. 'So why are you doing such hard subjects?'

I shrug. I don't find science that hard, but if you say that people just think you're weird. I go for the safe reply: 'I want to do engineering at uni and they say studying these will help. Assuming I pass my Highers, of course.' I wish there was some wood around to touch. Not that I'm superstitious.

She nods. 'Bloody annoying, isn't it? First they say work hard in Fifth Year 'cause it's those results that count for university entrance. Then they say, by the way, if you want to do well at uni, better work hard in Sixth Year, too. And don't think it's going to be easy when you get to uni, because it isn't. It's going to be even harder.' She shakes her head. 'Honestly, they don't want us to get the idea life might be fun, do they?'

I can't help smiling. 'Definitely not.'

Then she stops kicking her heels and frowns. 'You know what I heard this morning? Mr Cochrane is leaving at the end of this term.'

I must look blank because she tuts. 'He's Head of Drama, you must know that. He always takes the advanced class. I wonder if they've started trying to recruit someone new yet. We don't want to have weeks without a decent drama teacher.' She has that look in her eyes that makes me glad this has absolutely nothing to do with me. 'You know, I think I'll go and find out what they're doing. I bet they haven't even advertised.'

She jumps up, as though she's going to march off to the school office right there and then. But the bell rings for the end of lunch and we head back to class instead, Lily still muttering about how Galloway Academy needs to sort out its recruitment systems and maybe she can give them some advice. I shake my head, but smile too. That was the longest conversation I've had with Lily Hildebrand, and it was okay. Interesting, even. Which is weird.

Lily

I don't know why I hung around talking to Tom Owen for so long. Or, more precisely, why he hung around talking to *me*, as I was there first. I was waiting for Gemma who had gone to see Mr Barratt about changing from French to hospitality. It obviously isn't going well, as she still hasn't reappeared when the bell goes.

I won't see her until after school now, when I'll have to choose between hearing how mean Mr Barratt is, trying to find out what's happening about Mr Cochrane's replacement, or going home to Mum. And I don't feel like going home. This morning the only words we exchanged were her saying thanks when I took her up some tea. That's why I was so pleased to talk to Tom. At least it stopped me brooding about her.

Talking to him wasn't awkward like I'd expected it to be. I wonder if he's changed, or whether I've been misjudging him. Gemma always claimed I was, but until now I hadn't seen any sign of that.

While we chatted, I'd been waiting for him to look directly at me. I wanted to see if his eyes really are the colour of sea water in sunshine, but we were sitting side by side and he just looked straight ahead so I couldn't tell. His hair is longish and straight, and unless he's looking directly at you, you can't see much of his face. Maybe that's why I've never noticed his eyes before. Maybe he does it on purpose. He seems like the kind of person who doesn't want to be noticed.

He definitely makes an effort with his sister, though. I appreciate that. I've no time for siblings who think they're put on earth purely to fight each other. I might not hero-worship Jonathan the way I did when I was little, but he's okay. And Corinne's only eight years older than me, but she's been like an extra-sympathetic, extra-interested second mother – or only mother these days, it feels like.

Speaking of which, Mum isn't in when I get home. I tell myself this is a good sign. I don't think she's been out of the house for days. Annoyingly, Heather *is* there. She does the laundry and some cleaning for us – definitely a good thing now that Mum is doing practically nothing, but she always makes me feel like I'm a bit in the way.

I grab a yoghurt drink from the fridge and escape out into the garden. Later, when Mum comes back, I ask her where she's been.

'For a walk,' she says vaguely.

I say, 'If you'd waited 'til I got home, we could have gone together. We could have done that walk towards Dundress. I haven't done it for ages.'

She murmurs something and drifts off. It's a good idea though. I'll suggest it to her again soon, when I'm not so busy with the gala and the regatta and everything. I haven't got round to speaking to Corinne or Jonathan about her, but maybe I don't need to. I've got this.

Lily

The next time Tom Owen takes me sailing it's raining; that warm summer rain that you almost don't mind. Life feels different out here on the water. The light's different, the smell of the mud and salt are all around, and the only sound is of the wind in the rigging.

Tom is right: I really should have tried sailing before. Our house backs on to the estuary, but my parents have the big bedroom at the back with the bay window and all the amazing views of the water. Jonathan and Corrine and I have the rooms at the front, looking towards the town. Maybe that's why I've always gone in that direction.

'You need to concentrate,' snaps Tom, bringing me back to the present. 'This time you're in charge of the tiller *and* the sail. If you don't watch out the sail will go slack, like that, and then you drift and if the wind catches it the other wa– Watch out!'

I duck just in time and he puts up a hand to protect himself. It's pretty impressive, the way he does that. I'm sure I would have needed to look at the boom, and then I wouldn't have been looking at all the other things that I need to concentrate on.

'It's the current as well, it's confusing me,' I say, as the sail flaps and we lose speed. When you're on shore, you don't realise how fast the river moves out here midstream. The tide is going out too, which makes it worse.

'It was you who wanted to come out just now. I said conditions were difficult.'

I shrug. It was his idea I should learn, and if I'd gone home I'd have had to try and get Mum out of the house, like I'd promised myself I would. Sailing had been the easier option.

'You said the rain didn't matter, we'd get wet one way or the other anyway.'

'The rain isn't the problem, it's the tide that makes things difficult.' Tom pushes back sodden hair with the side of his arm, narrows his eyes as he judges the current and wind direction, and then goes back into instructor mode.

Who would have thought there was so much to remember, just to keep some fibreglass and canvas going in the direction you want? And Tom is a bit of a bully, making me do the same thing over and over, tacking across the estuary, going gradually farther out to sea as the falling tide begins to reveal the mud banks and narrow the amount of water we have to play with.

'I think you're getting the hang of it,' he says after what feels like hours, but is maybe only one. My shoulders are sore and my hands practically numb inside the useless gloves he's given me. I don't know if he's impressed with what I've learnt, or derisive at my slowness. He doesn't seem to do praise. 'Do you want to stop now?'

'Sure.'

I'm relieved I haven't had to suggest it myself.

'You go and sit near the front, down there.' He takes the tiller without giving me much choice. 'We could go out a bit farther, to the Flett Islands, if you want?'

'Well …' I'd assumed we'd just head back in, but the rain has stopped and the sun's coming through, all gold and hazy. 'Yeah, why not?'

The way he handles the boat, it's as though it's part of him. He doesn't clamber clumsily about like I did, just leans to one side or the other, scanning the water, watching the sail. Suddenly we're out in the open sea, not exactly skimming over the waves (this is a Topper, after all, whose closest relative is probably a bathtub) but picking up speed in a way that makes my heart lighter.

The Flett Islands are rocky outcrops, one or two big enough to have a few sheep on them. They're not that far from the shore, but in the early evening sunshine they look remote and beautiful.

'I haven't been out here for years,' I say.

'Not many people come. A few kayakers, the occasional motorboat. You're not supposed to land during the bird-nesting season, but it's okay at this time of year.' He turns into a sheltered bay, hidden from the landward side. 'You want to go ashore?'

'Why not?' I say again. I feel freer, childlike even. Maybe it's because the last time I was here was for a family picnic, when I was tiny and my family actually did things like picnics together. Or maybe it's because, for once, I'm not the one in charge.

I almost expect Tom to take my hand after we've pulled the boat up onto the shingle, and tell me to be careful of slipping on the rocks. He doesn't. He strides ahead, over the rocks and onto the short, springy grass. A couple of sheep turn and stare at us, then lumber away. 'The view's pretty good from the top,' he says.

He certainly isn't going to be polite and wait for me. He moves quickly and easily, graceful and sure-footed, while I slither around behind him. My trainers are wet from the sea water and really don't have a very good grip. Which reminds me: I really should get some wet shoes. Trainers are not ideal for sailing.

When I get to the top, Tom's already sitting on the damp grass, his arms around his bent knees, looking out towards the open sea. I drop down beside him.

'Sarah used to like it here,' he says. 'We used to have races up to the top. She often won. She could run like a hill goat, Dad said.'

I watch as a yacht sails past in the distance, its sails impossibly white in the sunshine.

'What's wrong with her?' I ask. He turns and glares at me. Maybe it isn't the most tactful thing to say, but hey, he raised the topic.

'They say it's Chronic Fatigue Syndrome, but no one really knows what's causing it.'

'But haven't they done tests? I mean, they can find out anything these days …' I remember Gemma saying Sarah was always at the hospital.

'I said they don't know.' Those lovely sea-blue eyes are looking at me, but their expression is cold. 'The tests prove all the things it *isn't*. It isn't multiple sclerosis, or rheumatoid arthritis, or cancer.'

'Well, that's … good?'

'But she's still not well! Have you seen her recently? She's stick thin. Some days she can hardly get out of bed. Why can't they *do* something?'

'I'm sorry,' I say. I feel helpless, which I hate. I think of Mum, who doesn't always get out of bed either, and then push the thought away.

'Why should you be sorry? It's not your fault.' Tom pulls his knees closer to his chest and looks out at the horizon. 'And actually, you've helped a bit. She's been better this week. She's really keen on designing the flyer, it's given her an interest that for once hasn't totally exhausted her.'

'I'm glad.'

He shrugs and stands up. 'We should be getting back.'

'Do you want me to sail?'

He snorts. 'Not if we want to get home this evening. Even though the wind has turned onshore, the tide is still against us. It'll be pretty tricky.'

'Fine, you do it then.'

It's quite nice sitting back, watching him work. I trail one hand over the side of the boat, thinking about nothing but the hiss of the water and the crack of the sail.

His hair is drying now, all wild and slightly wavy. When the sun catches it, the dirty blonde seems to blaze red and gold. His thin face is totally focussed, concentrating on what he's doing, not caring who's watching. It makes me realise how often the stuff Jamie used to do was done *because* people were watching.

I banish stupid bloody Jamie from my mind and concentrate on Tom. Why had I never realised before that he was worth looking at?

Tom

I'm sort of getting to like Lily Hildebrand. We'll never be great friends or anything, but you have to admire her energy. She listens to instructions, which is a surprise, and learns quickly. She glares and grumbles when I tell her how to handle the boat, but she does it. And she's sympathetic about Sarah. Not in a soppy oh-life-is-so-sad way, but like she's interested. On the Friday afternoon she even asks if she can come home with me after school and see how Sarah is getting on with the flyer. I don't know if Gemma put her up to it, knowing how Sarah feels about Lily, but it doesn't matter. The main thing is she's coming.

I text Sarah to give her some warning. She'll hate it if her heroine appears and finds her in pyjamas. She's got dressed every day this week, but I don't want this to be the day she starts flagging.

She texts back *Great. I think.* which sounds fairly positive to me.

Gemma, Lily and I walk back together. I don't need to say much because Gemma is stressing out. 'Why do I need to learn to drive now? I don't see the point. I can walk into town if I need to.'

'Or cycle,' says Lily.

'I don't like cycling. I never feel safe.'

'I can't wait to learn to drive,' says Lily. 'You're lucky your birthday is so early in the year, I'm not seventeen until September. It's so unfair.'

'Tom's seventeen and he isn't learning.'

Gemma's biting her lip and looking like an anxious rabbit.

'Actually,' I say, 'I had my first lesson this week.' I'm surprised she didn't see the car outside our house.

She frowns at her feet. 'Dad took me out in the supermarket car park last night after it closed, to show me the basics. It was awful. Cars are really complicated, you have to think of all sorts of things at once.'

I try to be positive. 'It's not that bad. It'll get easier the more you do it.'

Gemma ignores the encouragement. 'The driving was just about okay but I couldn't get the hang of starting and stopping.'

'Could be a bit of a problem then,' says Lily, smirking.

'You know what?' Gemma says abruptly. 'I'm just going to say to Dad I won't do it. They won't want to throw money away on it when I'm so useless, will they? It's only sensible.'

'But you need to learn to drive,' says Lily. 'It's a life skill.'

'I can learn later, when I'm older.'

Lily's having none of that. 'Better to learn now, before you go off to uni in a year. Get it out of the way.'

'I wish I wasn't seventeen,' says Gemma. 'It's really unfair to expect me to do things just because I'm older. Did you know a car counts as a dangerous weapon? You can kill people with one.'

Lily rolls her eyes. 'Never.'

'It's all right for you. You're not scared of anything.'

'And here we are,' I say loudly as we reach the drive to my house. 'Are you coming in Gemma?'

She thinks about it for half a second. 'No, I don't think so, thanks. I should take Toby for a walk. And I'm going to work out what to say to my parents when they get home, about how dangerous driving is. It's bad for the environment, too.'

Lily and I exchange a look of shared amusement. Honestly, when Gemma is on a roll like this, she's something else.

I push open the front door, trying not to think how different it is to the massive door of Lily's house, with its fan-shaped window above and antique lamps on either side. 'I'm home,' I shout, just in case Sarah hasn't realised. She's home alone today as it's one of Mum's work days.

Sarah doesn't come to greet us, which isn't surprising.

I lead Lily into the sitting room which, like every other house in the street, has double doors opening into the dining room at the back. Sarah is sitting at the dining table with her laptop in front of her like a shield. She's let her hair fall over her face and only manages an exhalation of breath as a greeting.

Lily doesn't let that put her off. 'Hi Sarah! Do you remember me? I'm Lily. I'm a friend of Gemma and, er, Tom.'

Sarah ducks her head in acknowledgement. As though she doesn't know who Lily is – as though anyone in the whole of Newton St Cuthbert doesn't know.

'Tom says you've been working on some designs for the leaflet. Can I have a look? Alice Beaumont was supposed to be doing something, but she hasn't lifted a finger. Plus I've thought of something else we could include ...'

She slides onto a chair beside Sarah and examines the screen. Honestly, with someone like that, even Sarah can't be shy for long. Lily's friendly and funny and keen, and really appreciative of the work Sarah has done, so one-word answers soon become two, three, then whole sentences.

I decide to leave them to it. I'm doing enough for this bloody gala as it is. I pick up one of the sample flyers Sarah has printed out to have a quick look before I make my exit. It's the first time I've looked beyond the lettering and pictures and read the list of all the things we're apparently doing during Gala Week.

The floor seems to give a little lurch as I take it all in. Not even Lily would be this crazy! But there it is in writing – stuff about the Newton St Cuthbert Talent Show, the T-shirt competition, wall painting, and then:

New this year! Our most inclusive Gala Parade EVER. We're looking for a:

Gala King (to sit alongside the Gala Queen)

Queer Gala King*

Queer Gala Queen*

Non-Binary Gala Monarch

*To apply for these positions, you must be one (or more) of the following: lesbian, gay, bisexual, transgender, queer, intersex, aromantic, asexual, pansexual, etc. BYO flags ☺

'Lily! Are you mad?' I shake the flyer in her face. 'You never discussed this with the committee. They'll go completely mental.'

She snatches the paper, looking annoyed that I've interrupted her conversation. 'Why should they? I'm just helping them out here.'

Sarah looks doubtfully from one of us to the other. 'I thought you knew,' she says to me. I remember her going "Wow!" when she first read the list. I'd just thought she was impressed with how much Lily had thought of.

'Lily, you can't do this.'

'Why not?'

'You just … *can't*.'

'What, you think we should just have a pretty girl standing there to be stared at? And that it's okay to exclude people – people like my sister, who by the way is a lesbian – because of their sexuality or gender identity?'

'No! *Of course* not. It's just …' I want to lay my head down on the table and pretend none of this is happening. How did I ever get involved? 'I just don't think the committee are expecting you to turn the Gala Parade into a kind of, I don't know, *rights movement*.'

'Well, everyone does have the right to be involved.'

'And the right *not* to be. Who are you to decide?'

She frowns, almost doubtful for a moment. Then says, 'We won't know if we don't make it open to people, will we?'

'This is going to cause a massive fuss.'

'So? Sometimes you have to take a risk to achieve things. Upsetting people isn't the end of the world.'

'Some of what you've got there doesn't even make sense! "Queer" is an umbrella term, so doesn't it already cover "non-binary"? Plus you've got the Gala Monarch on their own, while the others are paired off. And what's to stop non-straight, non-cisgender people just applying for the Gala King? Why do they need their own– What are you doing?' Lily had begun scribbling something on the flyer halfway through my tirade.

'Nothing, keep going, this is great.'

'Are you writing this down?'

'Well you've got a point. We need to re-phrase this. Why limit the numbers at all? There could be any number of queens, kings, monarchs, consorts, regents – Didn't I say we wanted to make the parade inclusive? We can have a whole inclusivity court!'

'A rainbow court?' Sarah says, tentatively.

'Yes! Perfect, Sarah!' Lily's pen moves furiously. The flyer is already unrecognisable.

I close my eyes. 'Lily, this is crazy. Believe me, Newton St Cuthbert really isn't ready for this.'

Lily straightens, tossing back her hair. 'You don't tell me what to do, you hear?'

'I'm not telling you what to do. I'm just saying this can't go out. I mean, at the very least you need to consult the committee. Didn't you say you would show them the flyer? And, honestly, can't you see–'

'I don't see how they can ask me to organise the flyer and everything else, and then object. They seemed pleased to leave all the teenage stuff to me.'

'This isn't exactly teenage stuff.'

She considers, eyes narrowed, cheeks flushed. 'You know, you might be right. I'd only thought of it as being for teenagers, because the Gala Queen is always a schoolgirl, but wouldn't it be amazing if we could get adults involved too?' She gives a little jump of excitement. 'I'll get in touch with Corinne. Maybe she'll have some ideas.'

This time I do drop my head to the table and bang it gently. I'm kind of doing it for show, to make her realise how mad this is, but I'm also completely out of my depth and it's the only thing I *can* do.

That evening Sarah is still pink with the excitement of the visit. I thought she would have been frightened by the argument, but she seemed amazed more than anything. In the end we'd agreed to do two versions of the flyer: one with the inclusivity bit (now including a section on our very own "Rainbow Court"), and one without. Lily thought this was ridiculous but I'd insisted. Both versions will be taken to the next meeting. I'm wondering if I can find a way of not going.

I watch Sarah closely for any hint of exhaustion, and I can see Mum is watching her too, but she seems to be floating on a cloud of excitement. If her jeans weren't so loose, and her collar bones didn't show through the trendy T-shirt she put on to impress Lily, she could almost be an ordinary teenager.

She's describing how lovely Lily was, how helpful and friendly. How creative and open-minded. 'And she's so pretty! She's got the most amazing hair and eyes. I wish I had dark hair.'

'It was nice of her to come round,' says Mum. 'She seems very good at participating in things. Is she the new head girl?'

'She will be,' I say with complete conviction. 'They just haven't announced it yet.'

'I thought they must have, with her being in charge of this committee.'

I manage to grin. 'It isn't actually a school committee, and she isn't in charge of it, although you'd never know that. She's just the one who likes to see things happen.'

'Good for her,' says Mum. Although she might not be so approving if she knew Lily was going to upset half the town.

Sarah says, 'There's going to be a talent show in Gala Week. I'd love to go. Do you think I'll be able to?'

Mum and I glance at each other. I think we're both worrying about a bad reaction after today's excitement.

Sarah's supposed to be following a programme called "Pacing" where she does a certain amount each day, and always stops as soon as she feels tired. It's meant to build up her stamina, but until Lily's design project turned up, we'd struggled to find anything she actually wanted to do.

'As long as you don't do too much,' says Mum.

'You can take it slowly and see how it goes,' I say. I'm not going to be negative when she's so happy.

If she isn't exhausted tomorrow, if this is finally a turning point in her illness, I'll be forever grateful to Lily Hildebrand, no matter how wacky and overbearing and annoying she is.

Lily

Gemma comes round on Saturday afternoon. I've finally found an opportunity to put my cookery plan into action. I've said I'll cook a special meal for Mum and Dad. Dad is actually home and I want to do something that'll make the two of them spend time together. Dad is a bit surprised at my offer, and Mum rather doubtful, but I'm pretty sure they're pleased, too.

'So. Salmon.' I look at Gemma for inspiration. 'What do you think I should do with it?'

'I don't like salmon,' she says.

'You don't have to like it. You just have to give me some inspiration for what to do with it. Let's look through some recipe books.'

The books aren't much help. Mum's cookery selection tends towards cordon bleu, with masses of ingredients and strange instructions like "make a roux sauce". We haven't got on to anything like that in our two weeks of hospitality.

'I'll try the Internet,' I say, and go to get my tablet.

When I return Gemma is sitting at the kitchen table, chewing her hair. I push the strand behind her ear – she really has to stop doing that. She narrows her eyes at me then goes back to paging through a massive tome on patisserie. 'I like this book,' she says. 'Some amazing cakes and tarts. Have you thought about pudding?'

'Not yet.' This is all much harder work than I'd expected. 'I'll do an easy starter, say tapas. Yes, Dad likes tapas. I'll go to that posh delicatessen later and get olives and stuff. I think I might go for some kind of Chinese dish with the salmon, they're always pretty simple, aren't they? And you can do a pudding from that book, something French.'

'I see you're going for the themed approach to the menu,' she says with a snigger. 'An all-around-the-world theme.' I ignore her and she carries on looking through the book.

'I wonder if I could make crème patissière,' she says after a while. 'I've always wanted to try that. And maybe choux buns? Or something with filo pastry?'

'Go for it,' I say. 'You're now officially the pastry chef. Or is it the sous chef? Anyway, you're in charge of pudding. Let's make a list of all the things we need. We can go shopping after lunch and then make a proper start.'

'We could use those funny orange fruits to decorate,' says Gemma thoughtfully. She's really getting into this! 'They've got some fancy name but they're also called Cape gooseberries.'

'Newton St Cuthbert might have gone slightly upmarket on the delicatessen front, but I think you'll draw a blank on Cape gooseberries.'

She carries on paging through the book, throwing me occasional glances. Eventually she says, 'How did you get on at Tom's yesterday?'

'Fine,' I say breezily. She doesn't need to know about the argument. 'Sarah's artwork is pretty good.'

'I know. It's funny, isn't it, that Tom is so into science and she's so into art?'

'Lots of families are different' I say, thinking of my own.

Am I imagining it, or is she mentioning Tom more than she used to? Later, as we walk along the narrow streets of painted houses to the supermarket on the newer side of town, I say casually, 'Anything you want to tell me, you know, on the boy front?'

She frowns so that the narrow space between her sandy eyebrows is one huge wrinkle. 'Er, boy? No, no. What made you think that?'

'You and Tom Owen seem to be getting friendly.'

She looks confused. 'Tom and I have always been friends.'

'I know, I know. But you seem to be seeing a lot of him just now.'

'Well, we live next door ...'

It isn't an outright denial.

I say, 'Yeah, well, but you seem to be doing more things with him these days.'

'Of course I'm doing more with him. You've got us all involved with this stupid gala. I'm spending more time with Sarah too.'

'Okay,' I say, but I'm not completely convinced. I mean, why wouldn't she be interested in him? He's actually pretty sound. And not at all bad to look at.

'Physalis!' says Gemma, suddenly.

'What?' It's almost like she's trying to change the subject. Only it sounds vaguely rude, and not at all the kind of thing Gemma normally comes out with.

'That's what they're called. Cape gooseberries are really physalis.'

'I'll take your word for it.' I giggle. It really is a weird name.

The subject of Tom is dropped. For now.

When we get back home, Gemma dives straight in to whisking sugar into egg yolks. She says, 'This is harder than it looks,' but her voice is happy; no sign of her normal anxious Gemma tones. I remember we used to have these baking afternoons when we were twelve or thirteen. Then we'd decided we were too grown-up for them.

'We should do this again sometime. Maybe invite some people and do a posh meal to celebrate the end of term?'

'Maybe.'

'Or a barbecue – that would be easier. A beach

barbecue for our year. How about it?'

'Lily! Believe me, we have *enough to do*.'

She's so vehement that I back down. I'm a bit hurt, though. I have all these good ideas, and all people can do is complain.

We set the table in the dining room, decking it with flowers, then serve my parents like they're in a restaurant. Gemma has to go home by the time we get to dessert, but that's okay. They thank her really nicely, both of them, and I'm hoping that now Dad is in a good mood I can have a little chat with him about Mum.

He actually comes into the kitchen with the dessert plates as I'm stacking the dishwasher. 'That was a lovely meal, Lily. I don't know what gave you the idea, but it was great.'

'I'm glad. Even if I don't think the salmon was quite right.'

'It was fine. I think your mum really enjoyed having someone to cook for her. It makes a change.'

This is my chance to tell him that actually it isn't a change for Mum not to cook, because she never does anymore unless he's home. And to ask why it is he's home so little. 'Dad ...'

'I need to go. I've got a call coming in from Paris. Did you say you were making coffee for us? I'll have mine in the study, and you can take your mum's upstairs. She's having an early night.'

'Okay, fine.' I'm not sure if he's trying to avoid

talking to me or if it just feels like he is. Maybe I should try harder to have that conversation, but he's still on the phone by the time I'm ready for bed. And when I get up the next morning he's already left.

Tom

Sarah still seems amazingly well. She's happy and doing stuff, even if she doesn't get out of the house much. Dad got her some design software, and she's not only done the flyer for Lily (both versions), but a poster too. We're going to show it to Simon Archer at the meeting on Monday. I'm hoping the poster will be something positive to counteract Lily's bombshell.

As Lily is at least partly responsible for Sarah's good mood, I'm trying to be grateful to her. If only she weren't so pushy! She phones me on the Sunday morning and says, 'How about another sailing lesson? I don't want to forget the bit I've learnt. And I think it'll be a good opportunity to have another chat with the commodore guy.'

'I'm a bit busy right now.' Okay, so I was already planning to go out sailing – but on my own, after the crowds have dispersed, right out of the bay and beyond. She doesn't need to know that.

'But it would be good for me to consolidate what I know. The kids training programme for the regatta starts the first week of the holidays.'

As if I don't know that. This whole thing is really going to eat into my summer. 'You won't be doing any of the training,' I say. 'You're not good enough for that.' If she can be blunt, so can I.

That just makes her laugh. 'I know, I know. But I'll be there helping out on shore, and I just think I'll be able to do that better if I have a bit more experience.'

'I don't see what difference it would make,' I say. This is the cue for her to say never mind, forget it. But of course she doesn't.

She just keeps going. 'It was you who insisted Gemma and I should learn how to sail. And as Gemma isn't keen, it has to be me. You can't back out now.'

'All right,' I say, not even hiding my sigh. 'I'll meet you down at the clubhouse at three.' If I keep the lesson short, there might still be time for me to go out alone afterwards.

'Cool,' she says. 'Now I need to find that Alice Beaumont and tell her that no matter how much she ignores my messages, she's still going to be the one running the T-shirt competition. Honestly, you'd think she'd be grateful I've done so much of the groundwork for her. She should be glad I'm not expecting her to manage the wall painting too.'

She hangs up and leaves me shaking my head.

While I'm walking through town on my way to the sailing club, I see a group of people from our year. I nod to them, but Mollie Douglas heads over to me, ignoring the fact that I've got headphones on and no desire to chat. 'Hey Tom.'

'Hi.' She's not one of my favourite people; silly and giggly and with the reputation as the nosiest girl in our year. I've no idea why she suddenly wants to talk to me.

She says, 'You and Lily Hildebrand got a thing going?'

I stare at her. 'No.'

'You certainly seem to be hanging round with her a lot. I wouldn't have thought you were her type. Jamie Abernethy was totally hot.'

I don't even bother to answer that. It doesn't matter whether I'm Lily Hildebrand's type or not – she's definitely not mine! Five minutes in her company is enough to drive me mad. Just when I start to think she isn't quite so bad, she talks me into doing something else she wants. Like taking her out on the water for the third time.

Mollie goes back to her friends and I head down to the harbour. I decide to use Dad's old Mirror dinghy this time. It's harder work than a Topper. It *might* keep Lily quiet.

It's always a pleasure to work with that old boat. I'm not surprised Dad has hung on to it, even if it is a bit rickety. I check the sails and attach them to the rigging. I've just dragged the trailer down to the water's edge when John Forsyth turns up.

'All set for the new training sessions?' he says, rubbing his hands together. 'I've been mentioning them to everyone I see and the response I'm getting is grand. It's a fantastic idea, so it is.'

'Mmm,' I say, guardedly. He's getting to sound an awful lot like Lily Hildebrand. Any minute now he'll be roping me in to do even more work. I look around hurriedly and am pleased to see that all the kids who need coaching today already seem to be out on the water.

'I've worked out the training times and Lily has made a rota for you and a few others. Pop up to the clubhouse when you've finished and I'll show it to you.'

I'm relieved to see Lily when she turns up. That distracts him and the two of them commune over the joys of getting the community involved and the importance of making lists. Eventually I have to shout to get Lily's attention. She's been absolutely no help setting up the boat. 'Are we going sailing or not?'

She laughs and tosses her hair, tied up in a high ponytail today. But she does leave John and comes to help me push the boat into the water, chatting like there's no reason at all for me to be peeved. And somehow, once we get out into the bay, I forget what was annoying me and relax.

The wind is strong, and easterly, which is unusual. The Sunday sailors are clogging up the estuary so I have to concentrate as I steer us out to sea. It wouldn't do Lily any harm to experience a capsize, but I don't fancy doing one with so many spectators.

As we get out to sea proper, there's a faint, white mist over the water. It makes sounds seem louder and distances hard to judge, which probably explains why there aren't many other boats out here. I keep the Marchbank buoys on our right, so that I have some kind of marker in case visibility gets worse. I expect Lily to comment on the mist, maybe even suggest we go back, but she doesn't. She holds the sheets as I instruct, her face focussed in fierce concentration, and when a higher wave than usual splashes right over her she just laughs out loud.

'You know, I could really get into this.' She sounds like she means it. Odd. Why would noisy, audience-hungry Lily Hildebrand want to be out here?

'How far are we going to go?' she says, a little later. 'You know, I've no idea where we are. We could be halfway to the Isle of Man for all I know.'

'We're sticking fairly close to the coast, heading west.' It's good that she isn't worried; the visibility is horrendous now. 'We should probably turn back. Ready to go about?'

And that's when it happens. The wind has been dying back, deceiving me. Now, just as I pull the tiller, it whips across the water and rips the mainsail from my hand. 'Watch out!'

Too late. There's an almighty crash as the boom hits the side of Lily's head.

For a moment I think it's going to take her right over the side. It could easily have done. As it is she gives a choked cry that isn't very loud, and slumps in the well of the boat, clutching her head.

'Ow. Hell. Ouch.'

'You all right?'

'No I'm bloody not! Shit.' She takes her hand away from her head and looks at her fingers. 'I'm bleeding. That really hurt.'

'Stay where you are.' The surface of the water is rippling again, a telltale sign of a stronger wind coming. I take a good grip of the main sheet, letting the sail take the wind, but not too much. The last thing we need now is to go over.

Lily is still cowering in the bottom of the boat, uncharacteristically quiet. Jesus, what if she's concussed?

I can't do anything out here. I turn the boat towards the invisible shore, and just hope we're beyond the sheer cliffs of Borra so I can find somewhere to land.

We're lucky in that, at least. When we draw closer I see we're well past the cliffs and I have a choice of little beaches. I head for the nearest, pulling up the centreboard and running the boat onto the shingle. I jump out to pull her higher while she still has some momentum.

'Okay, you can get out now and we'll see how you are.' I try to sound upbeat, but I'm really worried. Lily is never this quiet.

She uncoils herself cautiously and clambers ashore. 'I'm fine.' She straightens up and only staggers slightly.

'Let's find somewhere to sit down.'

The beach is deserted except for a dog walker at the far end. I take Lily's arm and we walk until the shingle turns to sand. Once the sand looks dry enough, I suggest she sits down.

'Let me have a look at your head.' God knows what I'll do if the injury is bad. It's ages since I did a first-aid course.

'I don't think it's bleeding so much now,' she says, touching the sore place with her fingers and then examining them for fresh blood.

I take the tie out of her hair so I can part it to see better. It's wet with spray so it's hard to tell what's blood and what's water. I prod tentatively.

'Ouch! That hurts.'

'Sorry. You're going to have an enormous bump, but I don't think it's too bad otherwise. I *think* it's stopped bleeding.'

'I'll be fine. I was just a bit stunned for a minute. Bloody boats.'

'It was my fault, I should have judged the wind better.'

'Don't get all apologetic on me. I'm sure if I'd been paying proper attention I could have kept out of trouble.' She's definitely sounding more like her usual self.

'Possibly. But I should have read the conditions. Just because there's a mist is no excuse.'

Lily seems to think the discussion is over. She lies back, pulling up the hood of her windcheater to pillow her head, and closes her eyes. She seems to plan on being here for a while, so I sit down beside her.

It's peaceful. I look out at the grey sea and white mist that might just possibly be lifting. The only sounds are the hiss of waves on the shingle, the distant calls of the gulls.

Colour is coming back into Lily's face and her wild hair is spread out over the hood and the sand. She's still for so long I wonder if she's fallen asleep. She hasn't.

She says dreamily, 'I like being out here. Far away from everything.'

'Aye, it's good to get away sometimes.' I wonder what she could possibly want to get away from, but don't ask. I just watch her.

When she opens her eyes I should look away. Staring at her like this is way too personal. But I don't, and after a minute she smiles, open and gentle. It's not often you can use the word "gentle" to describe anything about Lily. Then she does something even stranger. She puts up one arm, pulls me towards her, and kisses me.

I'm surprised. I mean *really* surprised. I should have pulled away at once. Instead I move in and kiss her back. What started out as a brief touch of cold lips becomes more.

'Well,' says Lily, when we eventually separate. She sounds pleased.

I sit back up, bemused. It isn't as though I've never kissed a girl before. But I didn't see that coming. I say something like, 'Um-hmm.' My brain doesn't seem to be working.

Then Lily sits up in one swift movement. 'Shit, I didn't mean to do that.' She's no longer pleased. 'I mean, it's not as if I haven't thought about it, but what about Gemma?'

'What about Gemma?' I shake my head slowly from side to side, but it doesn't seem to help. All I can think of is Lily Hildebrand, warm and sea-scented, *thinking about kissing me.*

'Gemma,' she says. 'She likes you.'

That breaks through the confusion. 'Gemma likes me? Are you mental?'

'You didn't know?' She looks sympathetic now, but not for a moment is her confidence dented. Does she really have no idea?

'Gemma has no interest in me. The only person she's fancied since forever is Jamie Abernethy.' Though god knows why.

Lily looks momentarily surprised, then shakes her head. 'Jamie? No, she's never had much time for him. And even when I was going out with him, she hardly said a word when he was around.'

'That's because she was probably too shy. She doesn't talk about it, but she always knows what he's doing, where he's going. Sarah says it's a shame, Jamie Abernethy is such a git.'

'Thanks.'

'Oh, sorry. But really he is so full of himself. For some reason Gemma doesn't seem to see that.'

'How do you know all this?'

I shrug. 'Sarah. Gemma tries to keep her in the loop, and she does tend to mention Jamie quite a lot.'

Lily shakes her head slowly, then frowns. The movement obviously hurts. 'I'll have to think about this, about Gemma ...'

'I don't know what you've got to think about,' I say, starting to get annoyed. Why are we talking about Gemma and Jamie Abernethy? I'd much rather get back to the kissing.

I put out a hand to push the heavy hair away from her face, seeing if she'll object. She does that smiling thing again, meeting my gaze, and I move closer, touch my lips to hers. Who would have thought kissing Lily Hildebrand would be so completely amazing?

Lily

When I get home from the sailing lesson I go straight upstairs. With Dad leaving first thing this morning, I never did talk to him. Maybe that was the reason I'd been so keen to get out of the house myself. If he could leave Mum on her own so much then why should I worry about her? She'd been better during his brief visit, and I hadn't wanted to be there when she slipped back into listlessness.

Now I don't want her to see I've hurt myself and start fussing. Or, worse, take no interest at all. So I slip past the lounge where she's lying, apparently watching a cookery programme, and make for my room. I call out 'Hi' and she murmurs something in return. So that's okay, isn't it? It's not like I've ignored her.

My legs are shaky, like I'm ill or something. It must be the shock of the bang on the head. I go to the bathroom to examine the bump in the mirror, but I can't really see anything. It's pretty painful, but as far as I can tell, Tom was right. It's not serious.

Not like the fact that *I just kissed Tom Owen.*

I've known for a while that I fancy him. Every time I look into those amazing eyes, it's hard not to feel it. And I like him, too. He's reliable, he isn't easily swayed, and he has opinions about things, like the flyer. I like people who have opinions, even if I don't agree with them.

But I hadn't meant to kiss him. Even if I'm wrong about Gemma's feelings and Tom is right – him and me? *So* not going to happen. We're too different. I'm too stroppy. He's too nice – although not in the spineless way I used to think. And I've no idea how I could ever have thought that he faded into the background.

Anyway, I'm not looking for a boyfriend. After Jamie Abernethy the plan was to be free and single and true to myself. And take up running and cooking. I need to stick to the plan.

But Tom can kiss surprisingly well. I mean *really* well. All I want to do is lie on my bed and relive the time on the beach. Which is pretty pathetic. I don't do the mooning over boys thing.

Fortunately Tom seemed to have the sense to realise this really isn't going anywhere, either. When we got back to the sailing club we were all cool and distant, didn't even mention when we might see each other again. Of course, I'll see him at school in the morning, but it isn't like we hang out together there. Things will just go back to normal.

Probably.

When I wake up the next morning, I find I have something else to worry about.

'Mum! What's going on outside?'

There's a truck parked in front of our house and a whole team of workmen are unloading a mass of metal poles.

Mum drifts from her bedroom into mine.

'It'll be the roofers come to set up. Your father has arranged to have the house re-roofed.'

'He has?' Why don't I know that? I like to know *everything*. 'Why?'

Mum looks puzzled, but only vaguely. As though this, like everything else, isn't really that interesting. 'He said it needed doing.'

'It looks fine to me. It doesn't leak.' Unlike the roof at school, which could really do with some attention.

'He said we need to ensure the house retains its value.' That certainly sounds like something Dad would say.

I was going to cross-question her some more, but she doesn't come downstairs before it's time for me to go to school.

The men have already got scaffolding up on the left side of the front door. They call out a cheery good morning. I answer, but I'm not feeling as cheery.

Mum's words hover around the edge of my mind as I walk the short distance to school.

Why does it matter that the house retains its value? Is Dad thinking about selling? It makes me feel cold. We've always lived at Bay House. It's the best house in the town. I love it. It's so central, so spacious, so pretty. Why would we want to move? Okay, it's a bit big with only Mum and me there most of the time now, but it suits us. We don't get in each other's way, and if Dad wants to impress people and entertain when he is home, it's perfect.

Maybe I'm worrying unnecessarily, but then again, maybe I'm not. I'll have to find out, and soon.

I'm already through the massive red sandstone gateposts of the school entrance before I realise that perhaps I should be thinking more about how I'm going to act around Tom and less about the roof. The problem is I have absolutely no idea how I *want* to act. And then there's still the issue of Gemma. Can she really have had a thing for Jamie all this time without me knowing? It seems unlikely.

I'm saved from having to deal with either of these problems when I spot Donny Miller sauntering in ahead of me, all floppy hair and languid movements. He's in my drama class and I think he might be gay, or bi, although it's not really the kind of thing you ask someone. All I know for sure is that he's got a rainbow badge that says "Love is Love" on his bag, so at least he's supportive. If I can get him to come along to the committee meeting tonight and support my inclusivity plans, that would be brilliant.

I also need someone else from drama class to start asking questions about Mr Cochrane's replacement. I've asked so many I'm now being ignored.

I shout, 'Hey, Don!' and hurry towards him, prepared to explain how he's going to use the rest of his day.

Tom

On Monday evening there's the meeting of the gala organising committee, the one I'm dreading because Lily is going to insist on introducing all her new ideas for the parade. At least, that was why I *had* been dreading it, until the kissing happened. Now I've got that to worry about as well. I've successfully managed to avoid her all day at school. It isn't that difficult. Our timetables are completely different and if I stay in the science block there's basically no likelihood of bumping into her.

By the time I get home I'm a) desperate to see her again and check whether I imagined the whole kiss thing; b) keen to show it meant nothing to me; and c) petrified that the kiss did mean something to me and nothing to her, and I won't be able to hide it.

I'm so gloomy on the walk into town with Gemma that she gives up expecting responses from me. I feel bad, but I'm hardly going to talk to her about Lily, am I? And then the thought occurs: What if Lily has talked to her about me? I study her cautiously for signs she's fishing for information. She isn't. I'm almost sure she isn't. She's still saying what a shame it is that Jamie Abernethy won't be around for the talent show, he's got such an amazing voice. Yes, it's still all about Jamie. That's all right then.

When we reach the meeting room, Lily is being her normal self, trying to change the way Simon Archer does things. She wants him to scrap the agenda because she says it slows things down. I think it's because she has lots of things she wants to discuss and she's forgotten to put them on the agenda.

Simon is getting that glazed expression adults often get when Lily is at her most insistent. He might have given in, if Mrs Hebden hadn't intervened. 'Nonsense, Lily. We've always had an agenda and we're having one today. If you want to discuss something not on it, you'll have to wait for AOB like everybody else.'

Lily glares at her, and then probably remembers she's going to have to charm the committee later on, so changes it to a grimace that's meant to be a smile. She introduces the boy she's brought along. It's Donny Miller. No prizes for guessing why Lily has got him involved.

I'm so distracted by all of this I forget to be worried about what I'll say to her. I slide onto a vacant chair with only Gemma between us. Lily looks around to see who's arrived and our eyes meet. We both freeze. Just fractionally. Hopefully nobody else notices. But it's there, that feeling, like a sizzle of electricity. I think I might be blushing and let my hair fall forward to hide it. Weirdly, she does exactly the same.

At least I've confirmed one thing: I'm definitely attracted to Lily Hildebrand.

My heart rate has plenty of time to slow down as the meeting drags on through discussions of pipe bands and a children's funfair. Then we move on to parking.

Simon's sidekick, another old buffer called Eric, says, 'We'll use the main area in front of the post office as usual, but we're going to need more than that for some of the key events.'

Lily jumps in. 'You can't use the town square as a car park. We need a proper outdoor venue for events. The square's the perfect place, right in the centre.'

'We don't have a town square,' says Mrs Hebden, looking confused.

'At the moment it's a car park,' says Lily impatiently. 'But what it should really be is the town square. And even if we can't remove the parking places immediately, for the duration of the gala we can take it over and use it as though it was a – a community space.' She looks around, pleased with herself for coming up with the phrase.

Simon glares. 'It doesn't work that way. Now, moving on – Mrs Hebden, you were going to tell us about the baking competition.'

Lily glowers, but gives up. For now, at least.

When he finally gets to the end of the agenda and says, 'Any other competent business?' it's her hand that shoots up first.

I groan silently and a few other people sigh and start fidgeting with their papers, trying to ignore her. They obviously don't know Lily if they think that's going to work. I feel a grudging respect for her. It would be much easier just to leave things alone, but if she thinks it's important to do something, she does to it.

'I've got some more suggestions!' she says brightly. 'Quite a few, actually. They're all on this flyer, advertising the new teenage events. Maybe you won't think it's necessary to discuss them all, but someone said I should bring it along.' She's speaking so rapidly that I realise she's nervous.

For a moment I think she might just table the non-contentious version of the flyer and all will be well. She looks at the two piles of papers, glares at me like I've been trying to sway her decision telepathically, and chooses a sheaf to hand around.

'It's a brilliant design, isn't it? Tom's sister did it. Apparently Alice didn't have time. Nice and eye-catching ...'

Simon Archer is nodding, probably hoping to get

this approved quickly so he can nip off for a quiet drink in the pub. 'Yes, yes, very nice.'

'It's cool,' says Alice. I'm grateful to her. She could have been a bit miffed about Sarah taking over the whole design thing, not to mention Lily's comment.

'What on earth is this?' Mrs Hebden's question isn't so much a shriek as a squeak. 'We haven't agreed to this! I can't believe I'm reading this. Gala King? Queer Gala Queen? A *Rainbow Court?* Lily, is this meant to be a joke?'

'No. Why would it be?'

Lily looks mutinous and everyone else starts reading their flyer properly, looking for the problem. It doesn't take them long to find it. Some look bemused. One whispers, 'What does it mean, non-binary?'

Mrs Hebden has gone bright red. Simon swells up so much I think he might burst. 'This is absurd. Appalling. We're not encouraging any of that kind of thing! Whoever heard of a Gala King? Not to mention … the rest …'

Most of the other old people, certainly Eric and two or three friends of Mrs Hebden, nod and shoot murderous looks at Lily. One woman ventures, 'Disgusting. Absolutely disgusting.'

Lily is now looking as red and furious as they are. 'I agree. The double standard in only objectifying a Gala *Queen* every year *is* disgusting. As for "the rest", I think it's an excellent idea. I thought you'd want to move with the times, be inclusive.'

'The town is very happy with the way the gala is.'

'You mean misogynistic and prejudiced? How do you know they're happy? Have you asked them? Have you asked any boys if they want to be King? Or the LGBTQIA+ community what they think?'

Simon is spluttering so much he can't get his words out. Donny Miller is in hysterics, which doesn't help. Alice and Kelly look surprised but not disapproving. I thought Sally-Anne might be reluctant to share her queendom, but she's nodding at Lily and looking really interested. It seems we have a generational divide.

'This is not acceptable!' shouts Simon, having found his voice again. 'Do you hear me? I will not countenance something so disgraceful being part of the Newton St Cuthbert Gala. You will destroy all copies of this notice.'

There's a silence and I expect Lily to moan a bit, and then produce the alternative version. Instead she stands up.

'In that case, I can't countenance being part of this committee. I hereby tender my resignation.'

She just manages to catch her chair before it crashes over, and she marches out. Gemma stands up and after a moment so do I. I knew they wouldn't approve, but I'm appalled by the way they've reacted. I'm far more on Lily's side than I ever was before.

I say, 'Maybe Lily didn't handle that very well, but she does have a point ...'

Simon ignores me and says, 'Any more competent business?'

Donny nudges my arm. 'Come on, let's go.'

As we leave I hear a rustle of whispers, one of the elderly ladies' voice louder than the rest, saying, 'Oh dear, oh dear, it's just not nice, is it?'

Lily

I'm so furious I'm shaking, actually shaking. Tom said they wouldn't be happy but I thought I could make them see sense. I never thought people would be so prejudiced, and act like that in public. Is that what Corinne has to put up with all the time? It was awful. Awful.

Once I'm out in the fresh air I lean back against the stone wall and try to calm down. I'm so stressed I'm feeling a bit breathless.

It didn't cross my mind that anyone else might walk out with me, so when I see the big main doors open I stand up again, ready for a confrontation. I can do confrontation.

But it's Gemma and Tom and Donny who let the heavy wooden doors fall shut behind them.

'Are you okay?' says Gemma, rushing over.

Tom pats my arm awkwardly. I start to feel tearful, which is really infuriating. I say loudly, 'They're all dinosaurs. Fossils. Idiots. I could take them to court. What they're doing, the way they're talking, that's probably illegal in this day and age. It's ridiculous. It's–'

Gemma says, 'Let's find somewhere to sit down. Okay if we go to yours, Lils? It's nearest.'

I nod. Now that she's cut off my tirade I'm too furious and confused to think clearly. I notice one positive thing, though. Donny seems to be coming with us. He didn't speak up in the meeting – well, they didn't really give anyone a chance to – but if he's sticking with us, I hope it means he's not upset about the whole thing.

Mum has already gone to bed, which for once I think is a good thing. I take everyone into the kitchen where she's least likely to hear us. Gemma sticks on the kettle and I slump down at the table.

'I did say ...' says Tom.

I give him a glare. Really, I so do not want to hear that.

Donny Miller is sitting in Dad's favourite chair, the one with the arms. He's stopped laughing now but he's still grinning broadly.

'Well?' I snap. It's not that funny.

'Well?' he repeats. 'What do you expect me to say? I had no idea why you invited me along, but I do now.'

I feel just slightly embarrassed. 'Sorry. They were completely out of order.'

'Aye. Completely. So what shall we do about it?'

I'm taken aback by both his amusement and by the question. I'd expect him either to be offended at the way the committee behaved, or annoyed with me for involving him. I'm too confused to work it out.

'We're not going to do anything,' says Gemma. She sounds quite forceful. She even bangs the teapot and mugs down on the table. Which makes me realise I should probably be the one providing people with drinks, not her. 'What can we do? We've all just resigned from the committee.'

For a moment I'd sat up straighter, as though maybe there was some heroic course of action. Now I take the mug Gemma passes me and say, 'Gemma's right. There's not much we can do. Maybe if you two had stayed ...'

'We had to back you up,' says Gemma.

'They were really out of order,' says Tom. And then, in case I think he's completely on my side, 'But I did warn you, this was never going to get approval.'

We drink our tea and polish off a whole packet of chocolate biscuits, and gradually I calm down. There must be a way of salvaging something. There must.

'What about the sailing regatta? We can't let them cancel that.' It had been such a good idea of mine. Was it all going to come to nothing?

Tom says, 'Oh, we can still do the regatta.'

I stare at him. 'How can we, if it's part of the gala? They'll probably cancel the whole thing. We're no longer part of the organising committee and I don't see anyone else taking it over.'

'We're still on the regatta subcommittee. You don't have to be part of the gala committee to be on that. John Forsyth isn't.'

I nod slowly. 'Okay, yeah. Yeah, maybe we can still do that.'

'Why would we want to?' says Gemma.

I've come back to my senses now. I say briskly, 'Because Newton St Cuthbert needs us. We set out to improve the gala. We're not giving up just because those people are idiots.'

'Maybe we can still keep the regatta going, but what about all the other stuff? The talent show and the art wall and the rest of it?'

I tap my fingers on the table, thinking. 'Alice and Kelly are still on the committee, aren't they? I wonder if we can work something out. It might be time for them to take more responsibility.'

'Good luck with that,' says Gemma glumly.

Tom is smiling like he finds me funny. When he looks at me directly it gives me a strange feeling in my stomach so I snap, 'What?'

'You don't give up, do you?'

'Of course not. Only losers give up.'

Donny pushes his chair back like he's ready to leave. After the first couple of remarks he hasn't said much. Maybe he is annoyed after all. He says, 'I should be off.'

'I'm really sorry.' I know I've already said it but I

feel bad about involving him.

'No worries. Can I take one of these leaflets? They're pretty good.'

'Help yourself. We've no use for them now.' I sigh. Sometimes it's really hard to stay upbeat.

They all get up to leave. Gemma gives me a hug but Tom just raises a hand in a sort of wave. Despite the smiles, and the way he met my eyes, it's obvious he doesn't want to spend any time alone with me. Which is fine. I've got enough to worry about.

Lily

I wake up feeling tired and grumpy. I don't bother making Mum a cup of tea, so I don't have to pretend to be cheerful for her. I don't even feel like having breakfast, which is completely unlike me. I make myself eat a yoghurt and then head off to school. I'm early and I have this vague idea of trying to track down Alice and Kelly and let them know what they need to do to keep the teenage side of Gala Week on track.

I sit on the wall near the entrance gates and wonder if it's best to wait here to catch them, or if they'll already have gone in. Or if I can even be bothered. I carry on sitting there, indecisive.

I'm starting to get pissed off with myself, never mind Simon Archer and his stupid committee, and have just managed to make myself stand up when Gemma appears. She's never this early.

'What's wrong? If you're still worried about me after last night there's no need.'

'It's not that. I tried to phone you but you've got your mobile switched off.'

I pull it out of my pocket and find she's right. Something is very wrong with me today. I switch it on and find it has practically no battery. I never forget to charge my phone. I'm still staring at it when she says, 'It's Sarah.'

'What?'

'Something's wrong with Sarah. Something bad. There was a doctor's car outside the house first thing. Mum went to ask if she could help. They said no, but they were waiting for an ambulance to take Sarah to hospital. It arrived really quickly, with flashing lights and everything. That means it's serious, doesn't it?'

I stare at her in horror. An ambulance? Hospital? 'What's wrong with her?'

'I don't know, do I? But Mum says she had a really bad headache and she mentioned … meningitis.'

We stare at each other. This is really bad news. Every now and then there's some scare story on the news about someone who only just survived meningitis, or survived with limbs cut off, or didn't survive at all. And Sarah is already so frail …

I swallow and say, 'What about Tom? Have you spoken to him?'

'No. I doubt if he'll come to school today. He and Sarah are really close.'

The first bell rings and we walk towards the entrance, not talking because there's not much you can say. I realise that being upset about the stupid gala committee was a complete waste of energy. That wasn't serious. *This* is serious.

Tom

I shouldn't have gone to the committee meeting. I certainly shouldn't have gone to Lily's house afterwards and stayed out so late. Sarah probably tried to keep awake, waiting for me to come home and tell her everything that had happened. She's been overdoing it. No wonder she's had a setback. It's my fault.

Apparently Sarah woke in the night with a headache. I didn't even hear her, it was Mum who got up. I don't know what time that was but by the time I woke the pain was so bad she was crying. Mum called the doctor who took one look at Sarah and phoned immediately for an ambulance. So she's off to hospital again, and this time with blue lights flashing.

Mum goes with Sarah in the ambulance and Dad gets out his car to follow behind.

'You could go to school,' he says to me. 'I can drop you there first.'

'I'm coming with you.'

I sit hunched in the front seat wanting to swear and curse, but keeping quiet because that will only make it worse for Dad. What could cause pain like that? A brain haemorrhage? Meningitis? Or could it just be a bad migraine? She's had those before, but nothing like this. I thought I'd read all the medical websites I ever wanted to, but now I get out my phone.

'Were there any other symptoms?' I ask.

He says, as though he'd rather not speak the words out loud, 'Your mum mentioned a rash.'

Shit. I spend the journey looking up details on meningitis. It isn't exactly comforting, but it gives me something to do.

Mum meets us at the entrance to the A & E Department. 'They've taken her straight for an MRI scan. They said to wait here and they'll let us know as soon as they can. She was feverish too. They were going to start her on an antibiotic. I think. I don't know ...'

We sit down on a row of uncomfortable seats, and wait. The place has been nicely decorated. They really make an effort with hospitals now, murals on the walls and everything. I don't care. The only thing I care about is Sarah getting better.

'I shouldn't have got her to do so much work. I shouldn't have made her do so much of the Pacing programme. I shouldn't have gone out last night. She was a bit quiet, wasn't she? If I'd stayed in, I might have realised something was wrong.'

'None of us realised,' says Mum. She sounds too tired to argue properly. They both look absolutely exhausted, their faces almost grey. Dad takes Mum's hand and they sit there, together, in silence.

Lily

Gemma phones me soon after I get home from school. 'It's not meningitis,' she says, sounding relieved. 'It's chickenpox.'

'What?'

'What Sarah has got. It's some strange complication of chickenpox. It can cause inflammation of the brain in immunocompromised patients.' She's clearly repeating something she's been told.

'Is it serious?' I don't think chickenpox is serious, but inflammation of the brain sounds pretty bad. 'Can they do something about it?'

'They're keeping her in hospital for a few days, but they seem relieved now they know what it is. I suppose that must mean it's not too bad.'

'Did Tom tell you this?' I say, feeling unreasonably jealous.

'No. Lesley, that's Tom's mum, told my mum.'

'But how would Sarah get chickenpox? She never

goes out.' I have this sudden worry that it's my fault. I'm the only new person who's been to see her in ages.

'Apparently it was going round at the school where her mother works. That's the only connection they can think of. Her mum's really upset, you can imagine. She, Lesley, has already had chickenpox so she didn't think it would be an issue.'

I'm appalled. Her mother should have been more careful. She must realise that Sarah is – what's the word? – *immunocompromised*. Then I feel bad for being judgemental when I've been one of the people pushing her to do stuff. Have I made things worse?

I want to text Tom to see if he's all right, but I don't want to intrude. I ask Gemma to let me know if she hears any more news.

Lily

Tom doesn't come back to school on Wednesday, which is the last day of term. He doesn't get in touch, either. It's not like there's any reason he should. We're not close friends and I hardly know Sarah. But still.

Gemma is quite preoccupied by the whole thing. I invite her round on Thursday, because we always spend the first day of the holidays together, but she messages back saying she's busy. I don't see what she can be busy with, unless she's busy comforting Tom, but I'm not going to be needy and phone her to find out. Instead, I decide to cross off something that's been on my to-do list for far too long: go for a run.

First I get kitted out in my running gear. I'd mentioned my get-fit plan to Dad and, as expected, he'd been willing to buy me anything I needed. He called it investing in my future; I call it buying me off. I'd even added in some wet shoes and he hadn't batted an eyelid.

Once I'm dressed, I do a couple of stretches. That's what you see people doing on TV. Then I do a bit of running on the spot, to see what it feels like. Even with a top-of-the-range sports bra it feels a bit bouncy. I'm not going to let that stop me, but I do put an extra black T-shirt over the skintight turquoise one, so I won't look quite so much like I want to attract attention.

One of the men on the scaffolding gives a low whistle as I appear beneath them, which was so not the reaction I wanted. What is it with this place?

I put my hands on my hips and glare up, finding it hard to identify the culprit in the bright sunshine. I shout, 'You do know I could do you for sexual harassment for that, don't you?'

The foreman cuffs a youngster at his side. 'Just whistlin' 'cause he's so happy to be alive, weren't you, lad?'

I don't believe him but decide to let it go. I set off along the narrow pavement at what I hope is a pace that's not too fast to wind me nor so slow I look like a total loser. It gets me as far as the corner by the tolbooth, where I have to stop and re-lace my trainers. That's what comes of wearing brand new kit, it never feels right the first few times.

I head through the school playing fields, knowing they'll be deserted. It's not that I'm avoiding people. I just need to get used to the new me first, before I exhibit her more widely.

I leave the playing field by the back entrance, jog through a very small industrial estate (Newton St Cuthbert doesn't really do industrial) and onto a narrow road that runs parallel with the shore.

It isn't a place I come often. It's a bit of a nothing road, neither pretty nor busy nor really rural. There are a few houses spaced out along it; smallish ones, not particularly smart. It's an odd place, when you come to think about it: so close to the shore but none of the houses seem to have a proper view of the sea. Bad planning on someone's part, for sure.

I'm running very slowly (okay, I'm practically walking) when I realise someone is waving to me from the front garden of a small brick bungalow. I wave back, intending to keep going, when I realise it's Donny Miller and he's coming towards me like he wants a word.

He leans against the gate post. He's one of the tallest people I know, and always seems to need something to lean on to keep himself upright. 'Wow, I'm impressed. You're a runner.'

I'd sped up to get to the gate like I really was a runner, but now I give up the pretence and come to a complete halt. 'Hardly. It was a resolution I made. I'm beginning to think not such a good one.'

'Maybe I should take up running. Get fit.'

'Donny, you're stick thin.'

'That means I don't need to lose weight, not that I'm fit.'

He winks at me, like he knows as well as I do that there are two meanings to the word. Donny's one of the few people who put me slightly off balance. I really don't know what to make of him.

He says, 'I've been thinking about that flyer you did.'

'Aye?' I presumed it was either that or drama he wanted to talk to me about.

'It was a good idea, to make the gala more inclusive. I've talked to a few of my friends. I think you should go ahead with it.'

I stare at him. It's not often people have bolder ideas than I do. 'We can't. You heard those idiots on the committee. They completely vetoed it.'

'But what could they do, if suddenly there were copies of that flyer all over town? Even if they don't change their minds, we'd still have got the idea out there.'

I narrow my eyes, considering our options. 'I suppose it's possible.'

'I know your sister,' he says abruptly. 'Well, not personally, but my cousin was in her class. She had a hard time at school. Small-town prejudice and all that.'

I frown. Apart from the Gala Queen thing, which had been mostly hushed up, I wasn't aware Corinne had any problems growing up. 'Are you saying she was bullied?'

He gives a languid movement of one shoulder. 'She never came out as gay while she was living here, did she?'

'Well, no ...' I'd just thought she hadn't been completely sure what her preferences were until later – if I'd thought about it at all.

Donny says, 'I think the more open we are about this kind of stuff, the better. And the gala is a great place to start.'

I nod slowly, distracted by guilt. Does an eight-year age gap excuse me for being such a clueless sister?

'So, we'll make more copies of the leaflet and hand them out, shall we?'

Now I shake my head, as much to clear it as to slow Donny down. I'm pleased he thinks my idea is a good one, but – 'It'll seriously piss people off.'

He raises an eyebrow. 'So?'

'I don't know ... If anyone does come forward, you know, for say the Gala King, they won't even be allowed to take part, which will be horrible. I can't see any way Mrs Hebden et al. will let us have a Gala King on the float beside Sally-Anne.'

'Then we'll join in unofficially. It's not like they can stop us tagging onto the parade. And we can just choose whatever titles we want. Come on – you're not chicken are you?'

I'm no chicken, but I'm starting to wish I hadn't run out in this direction. I don't mind upsetting people, but I really can't get my head round how this would work.

'Let me think about it, okay?' It's odd being the cautious one. Am I letting Corinne down by not agreeing with Donny? It's just that there's so much going on right now. The regatta. Sarah being ill. Mum being – not quite right. Tom not contacting me.

'I'd better get going, don't want to cool down too much.' I give a little wave and set off along the road.

I sincerely hope my memory of a lane that loops back to the main road is correct. I don't think I'm up to running much farther, and I *really* don't want to have to backtrack past Donny's house again.

Fortunately, as so often happens, I'm right. I can get home this way. I walk until I'm back on the main road, and then force myself to jog again. I even try to look like I'm enjoying myself, but I'm not sure I manage that.

Tom

I lie in bed until midday on Thursday. It's the first day of the holidays so I don't have to decide whether I can be bothered to go to school. I can't sleep any longer, but I can't gather any motivation to get up either. Sarah is still in hospital. They say she's going to be all right. Or at least, that the severe headache was 'only' caused by a viral infection and isn't anything life-threatening like a bleed, or cancer. I can't decide if that makes things okay or not. I know the hospital was all upbeat, but who knows?

I'm totally exhausted, physically and emotionally. I can't imagine ever wanting to get out of bed again. I don't even bother putting any music on, just lie there and think. I'd got Sarah involved in the things that tired her out, and made her more vulnerable than ever to infection. I'd been really pleased with myself, too. Excited by the chance for her to push herself.

To *push herself.* The very thing the doctor warned us could lead to a crash. Like she just needs to *try harder.*

What had I been thinking? About myself, obviously. I'd pretended I wanted her to be better for her own sake, but now I know it was for mine. It made my life so much easier when she was doing well. I'm completely, utterly selfish.

Mum thinks it's her fault, because of the chickenpox at her school. Maybe we're all at fault. Maybe this is going to go on forever and Sarah is never going to get better. If so then we're just going to have to cope. Looking after Sarah is what's important. But just now she's still in hospital so there's nothing I need to do. I close my eyes and hope I'll fall back asleep.

I don't. After a while Mum knocks on my door and comes in, looking tired and pale, but not nearly as bad as she did a couple of days ago.

'Dad's at the hospital now, but I'm going in after lunch to give him a break. What are your plans?'

With an enormous effort I push myself into a sitting position. She takes this as a sign I'm about to get up and opens the curtains, effectively blinding me.

'I'll, um,' I open my eyes experimentally and then close them again. 'I could come in with you if you want.' Then I would see Sarah, be able to judge for myself how well she really is.

'Thanks, but that's not necessary. If you could do a bit of clearing up around the house, that would be a big help. I was going to do that on Tuesday ...'

I keep my eyes closed so I don't have to see her expression. 'Okay, I can do that.'

'I'm just about to hang one load of washing out and put another on. Perhaps you could hang that up?'

'I'll try and remember.'

'And then you could go and see your friends. You don't need to be at home all day.'

'No,' I say. Lily and her ideas are a distraction that I really can't afford. 'I'd rather stay here.'

She says quietly, 'You're a great help, Tom.' I open my eyes now because I can hear she's coming closer. She hugs me, which I accept awkwardly. 'We do appreciate all you do to help. We're sorry you've had a bad time the last few days – or years, really.'

I shake my head and say, 'It's fine.' Which it is. If you can't change something, you've just got to get on with it. Mum looks like she might burst into tears if the conversation continues, and I really can't face that. Fortunately the washing machine beeps and she has to go and deal with it.

Half an hour later, I give an enormous sigh and swing my legs down to the floor. By a massive effort of will, I force myself out of bed.

Lily

Dad is in the kitchen when I get back from my 'run'. I didn't even know he was coming home, but I'm very glad to see him. He's making himself a coffee in that way he has of pretending it's the first time he's ever had to do it, so that someone will take over.

'I'll do it,' I say. 'I can grind some fresh beans if you want?'

'That would be nice. I don't know where your mother has got to, or I would have asked her.'

Mum is probably having a siesta, if she even got up at all today. She can't have been expecting Dad or she would have made more of an effort. Unless she's not even making an effort for him now. I shrug off the idea and concentrate on the fact that I've got my father to myself. Finally we have a chance to talk.

Once the noise of the coffee grinder has stopped I say, casually, 'I didn't know you were planning to have the roof done.'

'It's been on the cards for a while.' He's tapping his fingers against the kitchen table, a sure sign that his thoughts are already elsewhere.

I get out the espresso machine. 'This will only take a minute.' I measure the ground coffee and set it going. It smells delicious. 'This is a great house,' I say conversationally. 'It must be worth a lot of money.'

Dad looks at me in surprise. We don't normally talk about money, unless it's me asking for some and him automatically saying yes. I look back, trying to see him as a stranger might. He has the same build as me, tall and big-boned, and the same thick, wavy hair, although his is now almost white. He's still an attractive man though, even I can see that. He's nearly sixty but he has a restless energy that's completely different to Mum. What does he do in that life he lives when he's away from here?

He says, 'This house is an asset, like the London flat. You need to make sure your assets are kept in good condition, and work for you.' He sounds like he's in a business meeting.

'But a house is somewhere to live. It's not just an asset.'

'Nevertheless there's a lot of money tied up in this place.'

'And Mum and I live here. And you, too, obviously, when you're home. It's a shame you're not home more.'

Dad looks around at the beautiful kitchen as though it's unfamiliar. It probably is. Even when he's at home he spends most of his time in his study.

'Is that coffee ready? I've got a call I need to make to the States.' He takes the cup from me and before I can say anything else, he's gone.

So that's one more unsatisfactory conversation. I should just have questioned him outright, like I do with other people. But what questions would I ask? Are you selling my home? What's wrong with Mum? Why does the family not feel like a family anymore?

I'm not sure I want to know the answer to any of those. And I have more than enough to keep me busy, with the regatta and so on.

Corinne is coming home soon. Thank goodness. I've got lots to talk over with her.

I don't hear anything from Tom over the next few days. Not that I'm expecting to. I don't know why I even notice.

Saturday is a really miserable day. It's raining, not hard but constantly, and it feels cold in a damp, brooding way that's more like autumn than the supposed height of summer.

I think about going for another run but decide not to, as my legs are really sore. I wonder if I have shin splints or something, and nearly Google it before I realise that would make me as bad as Gemma.

Apparently Gemma has been doing some family stuff with her mum for the last couple of days, but she phones to say she's free now. I go over to her house after lunch. I glance at Tom's house as I pass, but there's no sign of life.

We chat for a while in the music room where Gemma's been practising piano. Who but Gemma would be doing piano practise during the holidays? I sit on the floor and stroke her ancient collie. He's still cute despite his age, with his silly tongue lolling out and his soft brown eyes.

'I wish we had a dog.'

'It's not all fun, you know. You have to clean up after them and walk them and everything.'

'We could take Toby for a walk now?'

'Actually, Mum took him out after lunch. I don't think he'll manage another walk so soon.'

'Poor Tobes.' I pull his soft ears and he gazes at me adoringly.

Eventually I get bored of being indoors and suggest we head into the town to see if there's anything interesting going on there. There isn't. Walking around in the rain is the pits, and makes me realise just how much Newton St Cuthbert needs some improvement. There are pubs for the adults who want to drink alcohol, and coffee shops for those who don't. If it's dry there is the play park for little kids, plus an open space called the Harbour Green by the river. And for us teenagers? Absolutely bloody nothing.

We walk along by the harbour, our hoods pulled up. All you can hear is the dull metallic clanking from the rigging of the fishing boats. They look awkward, half marooned in the mud with the tide so far out.

The harbour wall shows the unpleasant sheen of spilt diesel. The whole place is depressing.

'Let's go to the Town Hall,' I said.

'Why?' Gemma hadn't thought this walk was a good idea in the first place, and now clearly wants to quit and go home.

'Because there's an art exhibition on there.'

'Since when were you interested in art exhibitions?'

'It means they'll have opened that little café run by volunteers. It does the cheapest coffees in town, and the Women's Rural do the baking for it. Sometimes it's quite good.'

'If you put it that way ...' She trails after me, speeding up momentarily and then slowing again. 'But I haven't got any money.'

'My treat,' I say brightly. 'To celebrate the start of the holidays.' I'm not short of money. Dad has just increased my allowance. He says it's because we aren't going away anywhere over the summer, but it feels like he's salving his conscience.

Why does he need to salve his conscience?

'Are you going abroad this year?' asks Gemma, annoyingly chiming in with my thoughts. We've chosen our cakes (I go for raspberry cheesecake – fruit and protein, it has to be healthy) and found a vacant table. 'You usually do.'

'Well this year we're not.' I slide my coat onto the back of the chair, glad to get out of its dripping wetness. 'Because we're having all the work done on the house, and Dad's really busy just now.' That sounds plausible. I wonder if the real reason is that Mum hasn't got round to arranging anything. She's the queen of holidays in our family, she particularly likes the Caribbean, but this year I've seen no sign of the usual extensive research. 'Anyway, I'm going to be too busy with the gala.'

'We're out of the gala.'

'Yes, of course. I mean, busy with the regatta.'

'I wouldn't be surprised if the committee find a way of excluding us from that too. I saw Mrs Hebden on the last day of school and if looks could kill, I'd be dead.'

We sip our coffees gloomily. Even I can't raise any enthusiasm just now.

Gemma's phone beeps.

'Anything about Sarah?' I ask hopefully.

'No. It's just Mum wanting me to pick up some milk on my way home. God, my life is so exciting.'

It's no good letting her go on like that. I make myself brighten up and tell her about my run, and meeting Donny. That, at least, catches her attention.

'He wants to put the flyer out? He's mad.'

'Well, you know, maybe it's not such a bad idea. It's not just the Rainbow Court stuff on that flyer, there's also the announcement of the talent show and other events ...' When Donny said to put out the flyer, I'm pretty sure it was only the parade side he was interested in. But that was only one small part of my plans. 'Maybe we should put out an amended version.'

And then, like it's meant to be, Alice and Kelly walk in. Okay, it's not just them, it's a whole bunch from their year. I haven't spoken to them since the committee meeting because I'd got so distracted by the whole Sarah thing. Now I wave to them. 'Hey! You got a minute?'

They don't look keen but I've already pulled out the two extra chairs at our table so they can't avoid sitting down.

'You're still on the gala committee, right?'

'Aye, I suppose we are,' says Alice cautiously.

'Excellent. Now you're the only teenagers there, except Sally-Anne Mackay and she'll be busy with the whole queen thing. You're going to have to take on a bit more.'

'I don't think–' says Kelly.

'Not everything, I'm not expecting you to take it all on.'

'Well thank god for that,' says Alice, like she thinks she's being ironic.

'Look, how about just two events,' I say generously, 'one for each of you?'

'Well, maybe.'

Yes! That's enough of an answer for me to work on. I dig around in my bag and find one of the flyers, ignoring Gemma who puts her hand to her mouth to hide a smirk. I point to the list of events. 'Well, what do you think? The Design a T-shirt Competition would be a doddle to organise, and lots of fun.'

'I'm already helping out with the art wall stuff for the kids,' says Alice, 'which is proving to be an absolute nightmare. Did you know you have to put on a primer first? And there are all sorts of different finishes to choose from. And–'

'But your art teacher is leading that, isn't she? She was super-keen when I spoke to her.'

'She's getting me to order all the supplies.'

'Which makes this perfect. You can organise the supplies for this at the same time. I've costed it out, look. If we have at least fifty entries and we charge–'

'Okay, okay,' she says, sensibly giving in.

I turn to Kelly. 'And the talent show is a must.'

'It'd be a real shame not to have one,' she says cautiously. 'But wouldn't it be a huge amount of work?'

'I'll help,' I say happily. 'Don't worry, Mrs Hebden and the rest of them won't need to know, I'll keep in the background.'

Gemma gives something that I hope is a cough and not a snigger. I beam at the two girls. This is perfect. Two events for teenagers are better than nothing.

'We can use the same flyer, just cut some bits out,' I say.

Gemma says, 'And the part about diversifying the parade?'

'We'll have to cut that too.' I feel bad, but I haven't heard any more from Donny, which probably means he wasn't serious about doing anything.

'I've got a copy of the flyer on my phone. I'll send it to you, Alice, and you can remove the stuff we're not doing and enlarge the rest.' I wish we could ask Sarah to help, but of course we can't.

'Are you going to try and get back on the committee?' asks Kelly. 'It'd be so much easier ...'

'No way. That would look like I was sorry I resigned. Which I'm absolutely not. Don't worry, look at this as your opportunity to shine.'

They don't look happy but they're committed now. 'Like I said, I'll be happy to offer any advice you need,' I say as they head back to their friends.

I beam at Gemma. 'Excellent. That's one job done. Now I need to get back into organising mode for the regatta. I've been letting things slip. We're starting the training sessions on Monday. Lots of kids have enrolled. We can't let them down.'

Gemma looks up at the ceiling high above our heads. The front bit of the Town Hall is open all the way to the roof, three storeys above us, and lit by a large but grubby row of skylights. Just now you can hear the drumming of raindrops on the glass. 'The forecast is rain all week.'

'We can't let that get in the way,' I say bracingly. 'I'll check the detailed forecast when I get home. And I'll get hold of John Forsyth, see where we are with registrations. Are you finished? Do you want to come and help? You are on the subcommittee, you know.'

She shakes her head vigorously and says she needs to get home. That's fine. I can do this. I'm starting to cheer up at the mere thought of all the things that need to be done. This just proves I was right all along: you just have to keep busy.

Lily

It's about nine o'clock on the Sunday evening when I realise there's one thing I've been putting off: getting in touch with Tom. He's a key coach for these extra sailing sessions and I really need to know if he'll be there in the morning. I haven't had any contact from him since Sarah was rushed to hospital. He hasn't even responded to my message wishing her all the best.

I consider messaging him again, but that would be too easy for him to ignore, so I phone.

It takes him a while to answer.

'It's Lily.'

'Aye, I saw.'

He sounds tired and I feel briefly sympathetic. 'How are things going? How's Sarah?'

'She's doing a lot better. They think she'll be fine.' A pause. 'Or at least as fine as she was before this.'

'That's good. And you?'

There's an even longer silence, like he hasn't understood the question or can't work out how to answer.

'Tom? Are you okay?'

'Yes, of course. I was asleep. You woke me up.'

What is he doing asleep at nine on a Sunday evening? Nobody does that apart from my mum. I'm about to enquire further when he says, 'What do you want?'

Just like that, so blunt. Does he think I'm phoning because of the kiss (which feels like years ago)? As if I'm all needy and after a relationship or something. Like I've been waiting for him to get in touch because of that!

'I phoned because John Forsyth and I have been waiting for all the coaches to confirm they're coming for the training tomorrow, and we haven't heard from you. John says he's got twelve kids signed up so he's going to need at least four coaches, preferably six. He was relying on you to take a lead. A lot of the usual adult coaches will be at work, as I'm sure you know.'

'Is it starting tomorrow?' Now he sounds confused, like he's stoned or something. He can't be, can he? I've never had him down as a stoner. Maybe he's just out of it, like Mum – not a cheering thought.

'Yes, Tom, tomorrow. First Monday of the holidays? And then the following Monday, and the next. It was you who said they needed at least four weeks of practice before we could have even a mini race.'

'Did I?'

What the hell's wrong with him? 'Yes, you did. But if you're not up for it, forget it, okay? John Forsyth says he'll teach himself, if he has to, and I can help out. We'll manage.'

'Lily! You can't teach sailing!' He actually gives a stutter of laughter, almost like his normal self.

'I didn't say I could teach, just that I could help out.' He doesn't need to laugh. John Forsyth says I'm pretty good, for a beginner.

'Jesus Lily. You definitely need to stay on dry land. Can't have any of our learners being concussed by a boom! I can't believe I forgot it was tomorrow. Remind me, what time does it start?'

'Ten a.m. Haven't you been reading any of the messages? John and I are going to be there at nine to set up and be ready to register people.'

'I've had other things to think about.' He sighs. 'But I said I'd help out, and Sarah's not home yet, so I suppose I can. I'll see you at nine.'

I'm left feeling pretty miffed by the whole conversation. He might have made the effort to get in touch. And I don't see any reason for him to laugh at me or sound so put upon. I'm not the one who's forgotten their commitments. He said himself that Sarah is getting better. Bloody Tom Owen, who does he think he is?

Tom

Lily Hildebrand might be incredibly annoying, but it's actually a relief having something to make me get out of bed on the Monday morning. I sleep better after her phone call than I have done since Sarah went into hospital. When I get up Mum's just off to visit her, but says she won't stay the whole day. Dad's going back to work. Things are getting back to normal.

And even if normal isn't that great, it's better than the alternative.

Who'd have thought I'd be grateful for this bloody regatta? I get my kit ready and head down to the sailing club. It isn't raining but there's a mist over the estuary, making the whole place look kind of white and eerie. There's enough brightness for me to expect sunshine later, and there's a slight wind but not too much. More or less perfect for taking out a group of beginners.

My mood is immediately dented by the sight of Jamie Abernethy sauntering along the waterfront, clearly dressed for sailing. I'd forgotten he used to be a regular at the club. Presumably someone – Lily? – has drafted him in.

He waits for me to catch up, as though he takes it for granted I'll want to walk with him.

'I thought you were off on that school trip,' I say.

He smiles his self-satisfied smile. 'We fly out on Wednesday. I said I'd give a hand today, although I won't be able to do the other sessions. Forsyth seemed pretty desperate for some qualified tutors.'

'It's good of you to help,' I say, and I don't think he realises I've had to grit my teeth to say it. It's just like him to swagger in, give us the benefit of his expertise, no doubt get twice as much appreciation as anyone else, and then swan off again.

He is just such an arrogant git. I can't imagine what Gemma sees in him. Or Lily, for that matter.

'You're welcome,' he says graciously. 'It really is a good idea of you youngsters', to get a sailing event included in the Gala.'

Youngsters! How old does he think he is?

Fortunately we've reached the sailing club by now and he can go and ingratiate himself with Forsyth while I get down to the hard work of setting up eighteen Toppers.

Lily comes to help. At least she holds things or attaches things when I ask her to, and doesn't get in the way – which is about all you can expect of someone with her level of expertise.

'You're going to take them all out in Toppers, are you? Not the two-person boats – what do you call them? Mirrors?'

'There aren't enough instructors to have one per learner, which you'd have to do in a Mirror. This way we can teach more people.'

'How long have you been an instructor?'

'A year or so.'

'It's good that you've got the qualification.'

'Mmm.' I'm a bit embarrassed about that. I never finished the course because part of it had been when Sarah had a bad spell, but they gave me the certificate anyway. I bet Jamie Abernethy has ticked all the bloody boxes.

'I think it's great,' she continues. 'It's a pity there aren't more instructors.'

I just nod. I really hope she's not going to start a campaign for that. Or was she just saying it to keep the conversation going? I wonder if she's talking to me so she can avoid Jamie. 'At least you got your boyfriend to come down and help.' Shit, why did I say that?

'It was John Forsyth's idea to ask him,' says Lily. 'And you do know he's not my boyfriend.'

'Mmm,' I say again. I feel like a complete idiot. I might even be blushing. Jeez. I duck my head so that my hair falls forward. I should probably say something about the kissing. The longer I leave it the weirder it gets. I've been distracted by Sarah's problems, but I can't use that as an excuse now.

I should be happy Lily is treating it as a one-off, and just assuming we'll go back to the way we had been. That's what I want, too. But when she's standing so close, with her wild, wavy hair blowing about her face and that really attractive, curvy body so near I could reach out and touch her, I feel kind of ... odd.

I say, 'About the other day ...'

'What other day?' She tosses her hair back and looks at me with what seems like genuine puzzlement.

'When we were out sailing, at Borra Bay.'

'Oh, you mean the kissing.'

I want to say *Ssssh!* but just about manage to stop myself. I glance around. No one is paying us any attention.

Lily seems amused. It isn't surprising.

'I should have got in touch, but with Sarah being rushed to hospital and everything ... so ... I'm sorry ...'

She's taken a step back and looks at me with a sneer, not puzzled or amused now. 'You think I'm worried about that? I'm not. And why should you be sorry? I was the one who took the initiative. And, actually, I'm not sure whether I want to pursue this ... *thing* between us or not. If I was sure, I'd be doing something about it. You don't need to worry about me sitting lonely at home.'

That isn't what I meant! More importantly: *she's* not sure she wants to pursue this? I'm not sure either!

Actually, five minutes ago I was sure I *didn't* want to, that I didn't have the time. Now I'm thinking that it's definitely not just up to her.

'Fine.' I push my hair back and glare. 'You can let me know if you decide in favour. And then *I'll* decide whether *I* agree or not.' I pull the mainsheet taut and let it go with a satisfying snap that makes her jump. 'I'll manage the last couple of boats on my own. John Forsyth looks like he could do with a hand dealing with the anxious mothers.'

She seems inclined to disagree, and then she smiles, suddenly and brightly. When she smiles like that she's stunning. I'm glad she saunters away, so I can get my breath back.

She's replaced by Jamie Abernethy, who looks like he was intending to have a word with her but she marches straight past him.

'Have you come to help rig the boats?' I say. 'Great. Only two more to do. I'll take this and you can do the last one down there.' The last one is the oldest boat by far, and real stinker to set up. Serves him right for not coming to help sooner.

Lily

Well, well. Not only is Tom Owen pretty good at kissing, but he can fight back too! He'd looked quite pissed off when I said I wasn't sure I wanted to take things further. But he didn't just back down. I grin as I remember his fierce look, the way those amazing sea-blue eyes flashed.

I watch him as he instructs the kids, getting far more out of them than any of the adults, or smooth, self-important Jamie. Tom is competent but not overconfident. I like that.

I leave straight after the session, because I'm going to get Mum to take me to the new supermarket in Kirkdouglas. Exciting – *not*, but it was the first thing I came up with that she agreed to. And we can buy different ingredients there than at the tiny supermarket in Newton St Cuthbert, which will maybe inspire me on the cooking front. The trip is okay – as far as it goes – but it doesn't take long, and as soon as we get back home, Mum goes straight to the chaise longue to lie down. She doesn't even offer to help me unpack the shopping.

'Open the door a little, see if we can get a breeze through here.' She fans herself very slowly, as though even that is too much effort.

'When's Dad coming home again?' I say abruptly. The outing had been for her benefit, and she doesn't even seem to have appreciated it.

'He's been delayed. He's had to go to the States for a week or so.' Her tone is completely neutral, almost bored. I can't tell whether she regrets him being away, or is relieved. Doesn't she miss him? They must have liked spending time together at some point, or they'd never have got married.

'Why don't you go with him when he travels? It'd be a great opportunity to see places. You like the States, don't you?'

She just closes her eyes.

I persist. 'You don't need to be here for me. I could stay home alone, or get Gemma to stay with me.'

Still nothing. I want to shout at her to get some response, but what's the point? She has passivity down to such a fine art it's impossible to break through. For now I give up. I unpack the shopping then go upstairs and lie down on my bed. If Mum can't be bothered to make the effort, why should I?

Lily

I wish I'd taken Donny's number and not just given him mine. I feel I should find out for sure if he's serious about adding to the Gala Parade. For this reason and this reason only, on Friday I put on my running gear again and set off to his house. I'm now completely convinced running isn't all it's cracked up to be. My shins are still sore, and so far the promised endorphins haven't shown up.

To add insult to injury, there's no one in at the little brick house when I get there. I knock on the door, then walk around to the back garden just in case. Nothing. I try to think of who he's friendly with at school, who I can ask if he's away on holiday or something, but realise most of the people he hangs out with aren't in our year at school and I don't know them well enough to message.

Total waste of time.

The only good news is that when I arrive home, Corinne is there!

I sprint the last fifty yards when I see her car, remembering just in time to duck under the annoying scaffolding before I burst in through the front door. 'You're here! I thought you weren't coming until tomorrow.'

'And hello to you, too.' Corrine stands in the doorway of the sitting room, tall and slender and poised as a model. 'I wondered where you'd got to.'

I make a gesture to my kit. 'I was running. I did three miles.' She doesn't need to know I walked a fair amount, when there wasn't anyone around to see.

'Rather you than me. Do you want a cup of tea? Mum and I are just having one.'

And sure enough, there's Mum, sitting upright, with a beautifully laid out tea tray on the table before her. She doesn't look exactly animated, but she's smiling, pleased to see Corrine.

'I'll just grab some juice then I'll come and sit with you.' Mum's eye's narrow ever so slightly. I can see her thinking I'm totally going to spoil the ambience of the room, not stylishly dressed and carefully scented like the two of them, not sipping tea from a porcelain cup. Too bad. I haven't seen Corrine since we chose my dress for the school prom and I'm not going to miss any chance to be with her.

We can't talk about anything important with Mum there, but later Corrine comes into my bedroom. She raises perfectly defined eyebrows *very* slightly at the clothes on the floor and the piles of books on my desk.

'I've been busy,' I say. Actually, the books have been there so long I've stopped noticing them. Clothes I scoop up every few days and dump in the laundry basket. I do that now.

'How're you?' she says, sitting on the desk chair in preference to the unmade bed.

'Fine.' I roughly straighten the duvet and plonk myself down on it.

'*Fine* fine or "F.I.N.E." fine?'

Polished nails flash into air quotes around the letters, and I smile more genuinely. It's a throwback to when I wasn't allowed to know what they really stood for in one of teenaged Corinne's favourite songs. 'If you mean Fabulous, Imaginative, Noble and Edifying, then yes.'

'And if I mean Fatheaded, Inflated, Narcissistic and Egotistical …?'

I throw a pillow at her. Then, because this is Corinne, I let the smile fade.

'I'm *mostly* fine.'

She lays the pillow neatly across her lap. 'Have you seen anything of Jamie since he started behaving like a total wazzock?'

I shrug that off. 'I saw him at the sailing club. But that's not important.' I've totally forgotten about showing the world I don't care about being dumped. Obviously, I really *don't* care.

Instead I tell her about my ideas for the gala parade. I pull out one of the leaflets, even though we aren't going to be able to do all of the stuff on it. I'm hoping she'll be pleased with me for at least trying to be inclusive.

She looks at the leaflet and shakes her head. 'Honestly, Lily, you're basically talking about having a Pride march. Those are only big things in cities.'

'There are queer people here too.'

'Well, full marks for trying, but you can't be surprised the committee turned you down. Especially after what happened with me.'

'They're idiots,' I say. And then, because there's something even more important I need to talk to her about, 'What do you think about Mum?' I watch her closely. We've joked in the past, with Jonathan too, about how Mum has languid elegance down to a fine art. Now I'm not sure it's a laughing matter anymore. I feel guilty, like I'm giving Mum away. She was fine just now; she definitely made an effort for Corrine.

Corrine runs her fingers through her long, perfectly straight hair. 'Why do you ask?'

'I don't know. She seems ... she seems so out of it sometimes. Like she's not interested in anyone or anything. And Dad's away more and more, so I'm here on my own with her. And I don't know what's going on.' God, I feel like such a needy kid, talking like that. Like I'm only worried about them because of how it affects me.

Corrine nods, looking more sad than worried. 'That's one of the reasons I wanted to come home. Dad said something last time I spoke to him.' I've forgotten that Dad and Corrine speak fairly often, both of them having similar jobs.

'What did he say?' Dad hasn't spoken to me. I almost feel he avoids me when he's home, to stop me asking awkward questions.

'He said Mum's a bit down.'

'Well, I'm glad he noticed.'

'Of course he's noticed, Lily, don't be silly.'

'But why doesn't he do something, then? Why doesn't he stay home more? Him being away can't be any good for her. And now he's doing up the house, like he's tidying things up so he can ...'

'Can what?'

'I don't know! But it just feels wrong. Everything feels wrong.'

Corrine sighs again. 'It's not so simple. Dad has a lot of people depending on him in the business, and then instead of Mum being there for him she's just kind of ... absent.'

'And what about me?' I burst out. 'He thinks he can just leave her here with me? Doesn't he realise it affects me, too?'

'Lily, you're always so busy doing things and organising people, getting on with your own life. He probably thinks you haven't even noticed.'

'Of course I've noticed, don't be silly.' I sound sulky, even to myself, turning her words back on her like that.

'Which is good. Actually, I was wondering if you

could try and be around Mum a bit more. It is the holidays.'

She makes the suggestion cautiously, like she's worried I'll say no. As if I don't like to help people. She makes me feel totally self-obsessed. 'I *am* around. And I do try and look out for her. I made her go shopping on Monday. It would be nice if she was there for me a bit, too. If she took an interest in the things I do ...' Okay, maybe I am a bit self-obsessed.

There's Gemma with her lovely, interested mother and even Tom's mum seems normal – worried about Sarah, obviously, but still engaged with him. Why can't I have that too? I think of Corinne and Jonathan, away from home, living their own lives. I want to say, why does it have to be me keeping an eye on Mum? But it's obvious, really. There's no one else.

I take a deep breath. I can do this. 'So, what are you suggesting?'

Corinne nods like she's relieved I've shown willing. 'Let's play it by ear, see what we can interest her in. I'm here for a couple of days, we'll arrange some things that get her out of the house, see how it goes.'

I nod. This is sensible, a good idea. Corinne will get us into the swing of things and then I'll carry on. I'm sure it won't be that difficult. I'll make a plan of action – things to do together, Mum and me. It's going to be fine.

Tom

John Forsyth sighs loudly and looks at his watch. 'We don't have long …'

'This won't take long. It's just I've had an idea. I don't know why we didn't think of it before.'

It's the end of the second Monday's training for the new recruits and Lily has announced she needs a word with the commodore and me. John's invited us into the clubhouse, which isn't much more than a large wooden hut. I'm not looking forward to hearing what she's planning now.

She beams at us. 'On the Sunday of the regatta, when we have all the main races, why don't we finish off with a raft race? You know, where people make rafts out of whatever they can find and half of them sink. It'll be hilarious. We could have it as a kind of finale.'

'That's not sailing,' says John, disapproving.

'It'll be fun. People can dress up.' I can see Lily's really into the idea. Where does she find the energy?

'It'll bring in a whole other group of people.'

I shake my head. 'Haven't we got enough to do?'

'Raft races can be very dangerous,' says John Forsyth. 'No proper training, vessels not seaworthy.'

Lily puts her hands on her hips. 'Honestly, why does everyone have to think of reasons *not* to do something? Why can't you think of reasons why we should?'

There's another girl in the room. She's one of the coaches, about university age. She's counting buoyancy aids before putting them into lockers. Now she looks up and says, 'You know, I can see my older brother getting into something like that. His crowd are always up for something crazy.'

Lily nods triumphantly. 'You see! This is exactly what we need to get the twenty-somethings involved. It'll be great.'

I say, 'The twenty-somethings are already involved, they're doing a pub crawl.'

'And alcohol and water activities do not go together,' says John. 'It's really not the idea we're trying to project for Newton St Cuthbert's waterfront. Plus there isn't time to add in anything else at this stage. I appreciate you trying to do something for everyone, Lily, but I really don't think it's on.'

Lily opens her mouth to say something more but one of the parents comes in to talk to John and she's missed her chance.

I encourage her out of the building, just in case she's thinking of hanging around and having another go at him.

'Honestly,' she says, 'this is a really good idea. Why won't people listen?'

'John's been running regattas for years.'

'He's happy enough to have all these lessons bringing new kids into sailing. He's happy enough with change when it suits him. I'm talking about getting the whole community involved, making something really big out of it.'

'Everyone's entitled to their point of view,' I say, as we head along the path back towards town.

Lily looks at me as though I'm mad. 'Yeah, they can have their point of view. It just happens that mine is the right one.'

I can't help smiling. 'How can you be so sure?'

'If I didn't believe I was right, I wouldn't be saying it. Obviously.' But she does give a half-smile, like she realises how ridiculous she's being

'Lily, that doesn't mean it *is* right.'

'It is to me.'

'Obviously.' I begin to laugh. After a moment she laughs too.

'You don't understand,' she says, with a mock sigh. 'No one ever does. But don't you think the raft race would be brilliant? That girl could see the potential.'

'I think we've got more than enough to do with the regatta. I don't know why I agreed to be on the subgroup organising it. The number of events and races just seems to grow and grow.' I glare at her, so she knows who I blame for that. Thank goodness we're no longer on the main committee. I've got way too much to do as it is.

'Yes, isn't it great? And you know, now I think about it, a raft race could be more of a separate event, not part of the regatta proper. So we don't need to involve John, we can just do it ourselves.'

I shake my head. Does she never know when to let something go?

Now Lily has sorted that out to her satisfaction she moves on to the next thing. 'What are you doing now? If you're not in a hurry to get home, you could come to my place for a bit.'

She says it so straightforwardly, not like there's any agenda behind it, but I can feel my heart rate pick up. Lily Hildebrand is crazy and annoying and I don't know what's going on between us, if anything. So, to go back to Lily's place, to spend time with her alone ...

'I can't. I said to Sarah I'd go straight back and tell her how the training went. She seems to think these things are interesting.' Sarah's been home from hospital for five days and I'm trying to spend as much time with her as possible, she's so pale and thin and *bored*. That's probably why I haven't seen anything of Lily since last Monday.

Lily says, 'They may not be exactly interesting, but they are necessary.' She doesn't seem put out that I've turned down her invitation. Probably it didn't mean anything to her. Then she says, 'Hey, why don't I come home with you? It'll be more fun for Sarah if we both tell her what's going on. Especially as I can tell her about the raft race too.'

'I'm sure Sarah would love to see you.'

'And I can talk to her about doing another of her brilliant posters for the race.'

She takes my agreement for granted, and turns with me along the main road, heading towards our housing estate. To my relief, she doesn't want to talk about the regatta, or the raft race. Instead, she starts telling me about her sister who was visiting at the weekend, and how she (Lily) has taken up running. I'm surprised all over again at how busy and active she is. And how easy, how much fun it is, to be with her. She can be a total pain in the arse in a group, but one-to-one she's different. There's something genuine about her that I hadn't realised when I only saw her at a distance. She isn't doing things for show. She's doing things because she really likes doing them.

Much later, when she leaves to head home, I offer to walk back with her. I'm not being polite. I really don't want her to go yet. I want to spend more time with her. Just the two of us. Maybe see if I can lead up to a goodbye kiss.

But she says, after only a slight hesitation, 'No, don't bother.'

'I just thought ...'

'Nah. If you walk in with me I'd have to walk back with you to see you got home safely, too, and then where would we be?'

I go to the front door with her, making sure the sitting room door is closed behind us. I feel stupidly nervous, being this close, with something intangible hanging right there in the air between us. I try to think about something to say, about when we'll meet up again.

Before I've managed to form any words, Lily steps away. 'Well, I'll see you,' she says vaguely, and heads off with a cheery wave. I'm left standing there, wondering if there's something I've missed.

Lily

Gemma comes back from her cousins' the next day and her first words as she follows me up to my bedroom are, 'I hear you were at Tom's yesterday.'

'Yeah, I just went by to see how Sarah was doing,' I say, offhand. And I did, kind of. Sarah had been flatteringly pleased to see me. 'She's a nice kid.'

'I'm really glad you think so.' We're sitting in my bedroom. Gemma doesn't have the same reservations about it as Corrine, or maybe she's just more used to the mess. She's sitting at the bottom of the bed, her back against the wall and knees drawn up. She looks like a skinny twelve-year-old. 'You and Tom. Is there something going on?'

Bugger. I can feel a rush of heat to my face. I thought I'd been so careful, I haven't said a thing and I've seen practically nothing of him – apart from yesterday, when I hadn't been able to resist.

'No. Of course not. Why would you think that?'

'It's just …' She shakes her head and then smiles. 'This is really good.'

'Gemma, you're not making any sense.'

'You never used to have time for Tom. I tried to explain that even though he seems shy and – and boring, he's not at all. And now you've got to know him you've seen that for yourself, haven't you?'

'Ye-es.'

'And you fancy him, don't you?'

'Gemma, stop it, I don't know where you're getting this from.' I always have quite a lot of colour in my face, I just hope she doesn't notice it's now even higher.

'You fancy him!' She giggles. 'I think that's so brilliant! And he certainly fancies you.'

I start saying, 'Gem, don't be ridic–' Then I register her expression – amused and pleased. She really seems to think this is a good idea. She grins. 'I should have realised things were changing when you kept asking me about him. Why didn't you say anything? Did you think I'd mind because he's my friend? Why would I? Honestly, Lils, sometimes I don't understand you.'

'There's nothing to understand,' I say, peeved because I *was* worried. I'd accepted that she (probably) didn't fancy him herself, but I still wasn't sure how she'd feel.

She bounces on the bed. 'So you do fancy him? I knew it, I knew it!'

'Gemma.'

'This is going to be so cool. Do you want me to say something to him?'

'No I most certainly do not! Don't you think I can manage things like this for myself?'

'Yes, of course. But Tom's different. He's not ultra-confident like Jamie. He might need, you know, a bit of encouragement.'

'Gee, thanks.' Does she think I'm so scary I put people off? 'I think we'll manage fine without you.'

'What are you going to do?'

'I'm not discussing that with you,' I say with dignity. Actually, I realise I want to smile. To shout and laugh. Gemma doesn't mind if Tom and I get together, I'm fairly sure he's keen, and what I said about not being sure I wanted to pursue things? A complete lie! I'm pretty keen too.

'I wonder what he's like as a kisser,' she says thoughtfully. 'He hasn't really had that many girlfriends. He went out with that girl from Kirkdouglas when we were in Fourth Year, but not for very long. And he's kind of seemed interested in a couple of others, but nothing's ever come of it.'

I could have told her that he's pretty good at kissing, but somehow I don't want to. Not just because then she'll know things have progressed further than I'm admitting. It's also because, unlike with Jamie Abernethy, I'm not sure I want to discuss Tom with anyone else. This is special, between me and him.

Now I just need to work out a way for us to spend some time together. Alone.

Once Gemma has exhausted the subject of Tom (pretty quickly, because I refuse to join in), she says, 'So, tell me the latest gala stuff.'

'I'm not actually involved in the gala anymore, as you know.'

She snorts. 'That's not what I hear from Alice and Kelly.'

I wave that away. 'Everything's progressing well, I think. Did you have a good time at your cousins'?'

'It was okay.' She wrinkles her small nose. 'You know I don't really do little children. Auntie Faye kept assuming I'd be delighted to babysit, and really I wasn't. Thank goodness it was only a long weekend.'

'You could have said you didn't want to help out with the kids.'

'Oh no, I couldn't. Then she would have been upset.'

I shake my head. 'Even if you don't like it, there's money to be made in babysitting. Now you've got some experience, you could do more and get paid.'

'No thanks. Don't you think small children are, I don't know, just kind of dull?'

'Yup,' I nod. 'I didn't say it would be fun, just it's a way to earn money. And if it's in the evening they'd be in bed, wouldn't they? So you wouldn't actually see them much.'

Gemma gives a shudder. 'Rather you than me.'

'No way! I don't have any experience with little ones. Fortunately.'

'You have with the regatta.'

'They're ten and over. And I'm not looking after them, thank goodness. I just check them in and check them out. You know who is good with them? Tom. He's easily the best instructor.' Aaaaand the conversation seems to have come round to Tom again.

Gemma smiles like she finds me amusing. 'I thought he must be. He's been helping out at the sailing club for years. Shame we can't go round and see him just now, but I know his mum has taken him into Dumfries so you'll have to wait until later. Can you do that?'

I glare, but I don't really mind. It's kind of fun to have someone teasing me.

She carries on chatting. She's definitely in a good mood. 'Hey, one thing that was good about being with Auntie Faye was her cooking. She made the most amazing strawberry smoothies. Do you want me to show you how? You said you wanted to do more on the food front.'

'Could do. We'd have to go shopping for the ingredients. The strawberries in the garden are finished.'

'Let's go shopping then. And can I use your posh new food blender? That thing is so cool, I don't know why you don't do more with it.'

''Cause I'm not a very good cook?' I suggest. I've done hardly anything since she and I did that meal for my parents. I'm really letting things slip.

'Where's your mum? Should we ask her if she minds, before we start?'

'She's lying down. She said she had a headache. And she won't mind. When has she ever objected to you taking over her kitchen?'

'Your mum is so cool, she never fusses.'

I shrug and say nothing.

While Corinne was here Mum had been almost cheerful, but as soon as Corinne left it was like she just turned a switch back off. If I talk she listens but she doesn't respond much. And when I suggest we go out and do something she always says no. Then she goes for a little lie down. It's like just being with me exhausts her. Maybe, for now, the best thing I can do is leave her alone.

Tom

I look at the pile of posters Sarah has printed out with the words: *Ready to Raft? Register now oar miss out!*

'Can you give these to Lily?'

'I don't think there's actually been any agreement that the raft race should go ahead.'

'Lily says once the posters are up, they won't be able to disagree. And I think she's right.'

Sarah always thinks Lily is right. 'I'm not so sure …'

'I wasn't asking you to put them up,' she says, sounding miffed. 'I can get Gemma to take them along to Lily next time she sees her. Sorry. I shouldn't have troubled you.'

'Sarah, it's not that. It's just …' Mum and I have been careful not to let Sarah do too much, and so far so good. She's been looking better, almost lively, with a bit of colour in her cheeks. She's drawn her hair back into a high ponytail, like Lily often does, and seems alert and interested, but my reaction risks changing all that. She starts to look unsure. I say quickly, 'Okay, fine. And they are good. It wasn't the posters I was objecting to.'

She smiles shyly. 'Do you think so? I hope Lily agrees. I sent a draft copy to her and she seemed to think it was okay.'

'It's more than okay.' I look more closely. At the top is the gala logo (should we be using that?) and at the bottom are details of who to contact (Lily), then cartoons showing things a raft could be made of – fish crates, oil cans, plastic floats, old tires – just to give people suggestions. There's even an old bathtub, although I'm not convinced one would float. 'It's brilliant,' I say.

I just hope John Forsyth doesn't see it, never mind Simon Archer and his cronies. I can't imagine any of them being happy that Lily has gone ahead and done this without their approval. We're close to the regatta now. Maybe no one will have time to get a raft together and enter. That's the best outcome I can think of.

The other problem that I don't mention to Sarah is that I don't have any plans to see Lily until the next training session on Monday. Of course I could phone her and suggest I take her sailing again, or just drop by with the posters, but I'm not sure she'd welcome either of those. She was all up and happy about spending time with me on Monday, coming to see Sarah, but after that, nothing. Maybe she's decided that the whole thing was a mistake.

For someone who likes to express their opinions on anything and everything, she hasn't said anything about us – her and me – since that cryptic comment at the sailing club more than a week ago.

The very next morning Lily phones me.

'Do you want to go to the cinema in Dumfries?' she says, with no preamble. 'There's a bus that leaves here at four and one back just after ten. How about it?'

'Who else is going?' I'm a bit flummoxed by having this thrown at me so suddenly, just when I've been thinking about her. 'To see what?'

'There's some action movie on. It's a boy thing, you're bound to like it. And it'll be just you and me.'

'You want to go with me to see an action movie? Do you like action movies?'

'I don't mind them. But actually, I just want to go somewhere just the two of us, that isn't in Newton St Cuthbert, you know?'

The way she says it, so calm and crisp, takes my breath away.

I try for the same cool tone. 'So you've decided that you want to, er, go ahead with this *thing* between us, have you?'

'Something like that, yes.' She waits and when I don't answer immediately says, 'Well? Do you want to go or not?'

I'd kind of like to keep her in suspense, pretend I have something else on and that I'm not at her beck and call.

'Yeah, could do,' I say.

'Fine. I'll see you at the bus stop just before four.'

And because the bus stop is right by the post office, no doubt someone will see us getting on the bus together and then the gossip will be all over town. My stomach feels kind of jittery at the thought of that. Or maybe it's the thought of spending time alone with Lily Hildebrand. I definitely want to get to know her better. But I'm a bit uneasy, too. With Lily you never quite know what's going to happen. At least I'll be able to tell her about the raft posters, so Sarah will be happy.

Lily

I'm determined not to make any particular effort dressing up to go see a film with Tom Owen. It's not like I'm trying to impress him. So I don't know why I put on a skirt instead of my usual jeans or shorts. I know why I put on the fuchsia-pink plunge-necked top though. As Corrine is always telling me, if you have assets, you should flaunt them.

Sadly the word "asset" reminds me of the conversation with Dad and my worries about the house. But I'm not going to think about that now.

It's just our luck that, as it's the summer holiday, there are more than a few people from school getting the same bus. No one in our year, thank goodness, but there's Alice and Kelly (who should be working on the gala projects and not gallivanting off into town), and some of their crowd, and Morag Leslie who invited Tom to the sixth form prom. They all say 'hi' or nod, and then whisper among themselves and look again.

It makes me want to take Tom's hand, or put my arms around his neck, just to give them something to talk about.

I can tell Tom's uncomfortable by the way he lets his hair hang over his face. So he's embarrassed to be seen with me? Well, thanks a lot.

I choose seats near the front of the bus, knowing the others will head for the back, and we sit there side by side, not touching, not even saying much, while the bus passes through all the little towns on the way to the metropolis (not!) that is Dumfries.

'Well, this is fun,' I say.

'Hmm.'

'Yes, it is a beautiful day, isn't it? And are you looking forward to the film we're going to see?'

'I don't even know what film we're going to see.'

'It's something with Bruce Willis in. Or is it Robert Downey Junior?'

'Lily, there is absolutely nothing similar about Bruce Willis and Robert Downey Junior.' At least that gets him looking at me, pushing the long hair out of his eyes so he can glare. 'Do you actually know what film it is?'

'I can't remember, offhand. And actually, we don't have to go and see the film if we don't want. In fact, we don't have to stay in town at all. We can just get the next bus straight back and forget it, write the whole thing off as a mistake.'

He smiles then, sapphire eyes flashing. He looks

at me properly for the first time, at my stupid knee bouncing under my stupid skirt. 'You're nervous.'

'I am not nervous.'

'You are. Lily Hildebrand is nervous! Who'd have thought it?'

'Tom, don't be so ridiculous.'

He looks down at where our two hands are resting on the seat, so close to each other. Then he moves his hand and takes hold of mine, intertwining our fingers. 'It's okay. I'm nervous too.'

I make a huffing sound, so he doesn't think I'm agreeing with him, and hope he doesn't notice the little jolt I feel at the touch of his skin. I look out of the window but I don't take my hand away. And when we get off the bus on the Whitesands, we're still holding hands. That will give those losers at the back something to talk about.

The film is pretty average, as I'd expected, but Tom seems to enjoy it. Afterwards we buy bags of chips and walk beside the river to the children's play park, which is way nicer than the one in Newton St Cuthbert. The apparatus looks new and there's a multi-coloured fence around it. At least ours will be better once that wall gets painted. In fact, maybe we shouldn't stop there. Maybe we can introduce other things, like new swings and stuff. I'll make a list when I get home.

We sit on the grass and watch the muddy water rush by. It's different to the river at home, no boats, no smell of salt and the sea. It adds to the foreign feeling from the park and the strangers walking by.

The thing is, although I've now spent hours alone with Tom, we haven't actually spoken much. And we haven't done any kissing at all. This isn't going the way I intended.

'It's a shame we don't have a cinema in Newton St Cuthbert,' I say. 'It's ridiculous we have to come all this way.'

'They sometimes show films in that church they've converted into a theatre in Kirkdouglas,' Tom says. 'That's closer than coming all the way to Dumfries.'

'Yeah, but they only show those highbrow, intellectual ones.' I raise my lip in a sneer. 'Although, if they can create a cinema space there, there's no reason we shouldn't do something similar in Newton. We'd just need somewhere big enough to seat, what, fifty people? And we'd make sure we put on stuff people actually want to see.'

'Lily, you are not thinking about opening a cinema.' He looks appalled.

'Why not? It might be fun. Things are going to be quiet once the regatta is over.' I've really enjoyed being busy with preparations these last few weeks. Once it's all over, I'll be stuck at home with Mum. Taking on another project, one that is completely my own, with no committee to interfere – sounds like a very good idea.

I say, 'I wonder if any of the rooms in the Town Hall would do? The acoustics aren't great, but I can't think of anywhere else big enough.'

'Except the school.'

'Hey, that's brilliant! The main school hall is hardly used in the evenings or at weekends ...' I finished my chips a while ago and had been lying back on the warm grass. Now I make to sit up, enthused. 'It could be our Young Enterprise project for Sixth Year. What do you think? Pretty brilliant idea?'

'I've got a better one.' And he leans in and kisses me. Maybe he's only doing it to shut me up, but who cares? Tom Owen is taking the initiative, and I don't mind at all.

I remembered right – he is good at this. I forget about cinemas and parks and concentrate on the warmth of his lips, on the grass against my back and his arms around my neck, and the feeling of his thin body pressed against mine.

We kiss for, oooh, quite a long time. And then we lie back, holding hands, doing nothing more than looking at the clouds rushing across the pale evening sky. Generally, I don't approve of just lying back and doing nothing, but this is kind of nice. I'm sorry when it's time to walk back into town to catch the bus home.

Best of all, apart from the goodnight kiss, is when he says, 'Sarah has done some raft race posters. I'm still not sure you should put them up, but she asked me to tell you they're ready. I could bring them round for you to see tomorrow. Or you could come to my house?'

Yes! The raft race plans are moving forward *and* we have a plan to see each other again. Result!

Tom

I've decided not to agonise over the raft race or any of the gala stuff. The evening at the cinema was fun, and Lily and I spent most of the next day together, too. Life is good. I'm just going to enjoy it.

Or not.

I'm not even out of bed on Friday when my phone starts pinging.

Gemma, joint message to me and Lily: *What's going on? Mum's just been into town. Who pinned up all those flyers?*

Lily, joint message to Gemma and me: *What flyers? Am going to have a look.* Followed five minutes later by: *Oh shit. Will it help if I say it wasn't me?*

I join in: *What flyers? You mean the raft race poster?*

Gemma: *Mum brought one home. Been a few changes, but it's basically the flyer for diversifying the parade, like Lily wanted.*

I stare at the message in horror. I thought we'd

given up on that idea.

Lily was this you?

No, I said. Donny. It must be.

For a moment I don't believe her. She is always so keen on getting her own way. But then I realise that if she had done it, she'd say so. So on balance I probably do believe her. But still, she's not in the clear. It's her fault for starting it all.

I'm out of bed and getting dressed as fast as I can when Mum appears holding the house phone. 'It's Simon Archer. For you.'

I want to shout, *It's nothing to do with me!* but I take the phone and go back into my bedroom. Mum doesn't follow me but Sarah does, still in her pyjamas.

Simon Archer is ranting so loudly I have to hold the phone away from my ear. 'You young people have really overstepped the mark! This is outrageous … appalling publicity … Don't think you'll get away with this.'

'So he's seen them,' murmurs Sarah.

I let Simon carry on while I whisper, 'How do you know?'

'Everyone's talking about it online.'

I close my eyes. When Simon finally pauses for breath I say, 'I'm really sorry about this but why are you phoning me? Until about five minutes ago I knew nothing about it.'

'No one's answering the bloody phone at the Hildebrand house! It's that girl, I know it is, and you're one of her friends.'

It annoys me that he's willing to jump to a conclusion like that. I say, 'It's nothing to do with Lily or Gemma or me. You shouldn't just accuse people unless you have evidence. Maybe it's just a prank and it'll all die down.'

'Die down? I've had the national press on to me! Apparently it's all over Tweeter or whatever you call that thing. This is a catastrophe, a complete catastrophe.'

I try a few more apologies, and say again that it's not us. It doesn't seem to do much good.

He says, 'You haven't heard the last of this!' and rings off.

'Oh dear,' I say to Sarah.

She's sitting on my bed, but looking excited, not tired. 'I think it's funny. If it wasn't Lily, who was it?'

'I need to talk to Lily and Gemma.'

'Invite them here. Please. Then I can hear what's going on. After all, it was me who did the original flyer.'

I don't have a better idea so I message Lily and Gemma, then go to grab some breakfast before they turn up.

Lily

'So what are we going to do?' I say. Tom's parents are out and we're all in his sitting room, Sarah leaning back on the settee.

'Do we have to do anything?' says Gemma. I give her a dirty look.

'Simon Archer was apoplectic,' says Tom gloomily. 'I hope they don't go and cancel the regatta or something.'

It's good Tom has really got into the whole regatta thing. Everyone has, actually. We'll all be gutted if it doesn't go ahead.

'Simon Archer didn't mention cancelling it, did he? Not that it's his regatta.'

'But it is his Gala Parade,' says Gemma.

Tom sighs. 'This morning he was too furious to do anything but shout, but once he's calmed down a bit ...'

'It's ridiculous, really, isn't it?' says Sarah. She's looking remarkably perky. She's not worried about upsetting people, like Tom and Gemma are. 'I mean, they wanted the gala to be a big thing, that's why they were looking for extra people to be involved. I don't see why they're so upset.'

Tom looks at her like she's mad.

I nod. I know I tried to put Donny off originally, but that was a mistake. 'You know, you're right. They should be pleased.' Tom turns his look on me, and Gemma shakes her head. I continue, 'Don't you see? We shouldn't be looking for damage limitation, we should be riding the wave. Get out there, contact the papers, talk to the TV cameras.'

I can feel the excitement rising in me. This is the way to respond to adversity. Face it head on.

'That'd be brilliant,' says Sarah.

'You weren't the one who spoke to Simon Archer,' says Tom. 'I told you, he's completely furious. I think he'd rather cancel the whole gala than let a –' he glances at some of the new wording on the flyer Gemma brought with her '– a Pride Parade become part of it.'

'He won't dare,' I say confidently. 'Too much loss of face. Now, what's the best way to do this? It's not going to be easy, getting a whole new parade together in time ...' I chew my lip, trying to see how we can progress this. I'll definitely go all out for the publicity, but how can we make sure people turn up? Who do we ask?

Gemma gives a soft sigh and says, 'You did say it was probably Donny Miller who put out the flyers. Why not get in touch with him?'

'I've already thought of that. Problem is, I don't know how to get hold of him. We could walk out to his house, I suppose.'

Tom gets out his mobile. 'I might have his number. He was in my project group in chemistry and we all had each other's details.'

I'm a teeny bit peeved with Donny. When I'd said "let's not decide anything right now" I'd assumed he'd get back to me before taking action. After all, it was originally my flyer. Still, no point letting a bit of annoyance get in our way. 'Brilliant, you do that.'

I leave Tom to talk to Donny, who admits to putting out the flyers, is delighted with the impact so far, and is apparently up for doing lots of publicity.

'Maybe if we get TV cameras into town I can talk to them about the raft race too,' I say to Gemma.

Gemma scrunches up her face. 'Lily! I really don't think you should introduce any other new ideas.'

'Rubbish!' I say. 'And anyway, it's not a *new* idea.' She and Tom are being ridiculous about this. I wish I'd already put up the posters.

'I think we should leave it for now,' says Tom, who's finished talking to Donny. 'I think we've done more than enough for this summer. I'm pretty sure you could get the raft race and other stuff through next year. Let's wait until then.'

'No way, I'm not backing down.'

'Well, count me out.'

I shrug. I wasn't counting him in, he needn't worry.

I'll put up the posters later today. Simon Archer has already got his knickers into such a twist about the parade, one more thing won't matter. Plus I've just remembered John Forsyth is away for a couple of days – an excellent time to get the posters out there.

'Tell us what Donny was saying. I think we'll have to set up another virtual subcommittee, this time for the alternative parade. We can all be on it, plus Donny. How about it?'

Tom shakes his head. 'Seems to me Donny has got it all in hand, so we don't need any more subcommittees. Thank god.'

I give a little huff of annoyance. It's good that Donny's taken the initiative, of course, but it doesn't feel right, not being in charge. Maybe I'll get his phone number off Tom and see if he needs a helping hand.

Tom

'So, are you going out with Lily Hildebrand?' It's Sarah who's asking. I look at her blankly for a moment, having been distracted by other things.

I never even told her I'd gone to the cinema with Lily, but maybe she heard about it from Gemma. Or just noticed the way Lily and I are when we're together, which we have been for most of today. Even when I'm annoyed with Lily, I can't resist sitting close, touching her occasionally. And Lily seems the same, her hand just happening to slide over mine when she reaches for something.

I sigh. Haven't we got enough on our plates at the moment? 'Nothing to do with you.' And, actually, I don't know if we are officially going out. We haven't spoken about it.

I hope that if I sound irritated she'll let it go.

She doesn't. 'But do you like her? She must like you, if she invited you to go to Dumfries with her.'

So she did know about that. 'Who told you that?'

'Gemma. Why? Was it a secret?'

'No.'

'And you must like her a little bit if you agreed to go. Was it fun? What film did you see?'

'Yes, what film was it?' says Mum, choosing this moment to come in to the sitting room. 'And who did you go with?'

'He went with Lily Hildebrand!' says Sarah, eyes laughing behind her glasses. It is *almost* worth the discomfort of the conversation to see her looking so lively.

Mum looks vague. 'Lily …? Oh, that nice girl who has been working on the posters with Sarah? I thought she was Gemma's friend. Did Gemma go too?'

'Mu-um,' says Sarah. 'It was a date. You don't take a third person along on a date.'

'It wasn't a date,' I say, and then think of lying on the grass in the park, kissing. And hope to god I'm not blushing.

'Tom can't decide whether he likes her or not,' says Sarah, looking disapproving.

'Like I'm going to tell you either way.'

'Aw, Tom, I really like Lily! She's so pretty, and fun. She has amazing ideas. She *does* things.' Sarah makes herself sit up straighter, as though she can force herself to be strong enough to do things, too.

'Don't tease Tom,' says Mum, surprisingly taking my side. 'Now, what I really came in here to ask was, what did Simon Archer want this morning? He sounded a bit off.'

'It was, er, something to do with the gala.'

'There's been a big stushie,' says Sarah, grinning manically. 'Haven't you heard about the flyers and things around the town?'

'No. I've been at Gran's most of the day.'

'It's nothing, all calming down now,' I say. I don't want to get into a discussion about this. Fortunately she takes the hint and stops asking questions.

The whole weekend is exhausting. I'm shattered trying to keep up with Lily's arrangements (and watering them down where I can). I think I manage to keep everyone *almost* happy, but it's not easy telling so many half-truths. I knew getting involved with Lily Hildebrand would mean hard work. I just hadn't thought it would be this sort of hard work!

At least Donny has done the live radio and TV interviews – which he should do, seeing as he's the one who brought things to a head. Lily somehow managed to get on air too. They both seem to enjoy it. The weirdest thing is that, despite all the hassle and hard work, I'm actually happy. I'm happy because Sarah's having fun, I'm happy when I'm with Lily, and happiest of all when it's just the two of us. Surely things will calm down next week and we can get away, do something that isn't gala-related. Maybe even figure out the answer to Sarah's question: *Am* I going out with Lily Hildebrand?

Lily

Very late on Sunday evening, Dad phones me from New York. You'd think as he travels so much, he'd remember the time difference. The fact that I'm still awake, thinking about Tom and the parade and the regatta (and then Tom again), is beside the point.

He phones on my mobile, which is unusual.

'Your mother has an appointment to see the GP,' he says abruptly. 'Tomorrow morning at eleven. She asked Corinne to arrange it for her. Do you think you can make sure she gets there?'

I swallow down the rush of panic. Why this, all of a sudden? 'What for?'

'We've been trying to persuade your mum to see a doctor for a while.'

'Oh.' Nobody told me. 'Why?'

He doesn't answer. 'She finally agreed, but we're worried she might not actually go.'

'Why wouldn't she go?' I don't like this. I don't like this at all.

'She might ... forget. It would be just like her to forget to go. I want you to go along with her.'

'Dad! I can't go into the doctor's room with her.'

'You don't need to go in the consulting room. Just go with her as far as the waiting room and make sure she actually goes in.'

'Okay,' I say. 'But what's wrong with her?'

'That's what we're hoping the GP will tell us. So, eleven a.m. tomorrow, okay?'

I don't want to do this. I really don't want to be the one taking my mum to the doctor's.

I say, 'I wish you were home, Dad.' It's one in the morning, dark even on a midsummer's night. The massive house feels empty.

'I have work to do,' he says briskly. 'With luck, I'll be back at the weekend. You can text me, let me know how she gets on. Oh, and maybe you could make sure she has some breakfast before she goes out?'

We say a quick goodbye and the call ends.

So that's that. Apparently I'm now my mother's carer, the person who checks she eats properly and takes her to the doctor's.

This is ridiculous! I don't even know what's wrong with her. She doesn't look ill. Okay, she's thin – probably a bit too thin – but she still dresses nicely, she hasn't given up on that. And she's perfectly capable of talking normally to other people, like Heather or the roofers. Although … I know Heather has noticed things aren't quite right. She'd cornered me last week and said, 'Don't you think your mum's a wee bit quiet? I wondered if she was, like, no so well just now.'

I'd shrugged it off, because what could I say? Despite all the fuss around the Gala Parade, I had actually made Mum take me to Kirkdouglas again on Saturday, to go to a dress shop she used to really like and then a Mediterranean-style café. She'd gone along with it because I'd insisted, but I wouldn't say she'd actually enjoyed it. And I can't remember any other occasion she's been out since Corinne was home. She's even talking about having groceries delivered to the house.

With a sinking heart I realise it might not be that easy to get her to the doctor's surgery.

I see that Tom is still online, and turn with relief to type a message. Tomorrow is soon enough to think about Mum. I tell him I'll be late for the training session in the morning because I've got to do something with Mum. Afterwards we banter about nothing much. Every time I come up with a serious plan for something useful (like using my proposed cinema for a monthly open mic night) he shoots me down with comments like "And when Lily takes over the world …" so eventually I give up and we resort to trading gifs with each other. I've pretty much calmed down by the time I finally go to bed.

Lily

Despite the late night, I get up early on Monday morning. I do some stretches and think about going for a run and a shower, but in the end I just have the shower.

By ten o'clock I'm downstairs and have had my breakfast, but there's still no sound from the lovely master bedroom that Mum and Dad share (when Dad's home). I sigh. I go up and knock on the door. Nothing. I glance around the spacious landing, as though there might be someone there who can advise me. Of course there isn't. I'm home alone, as always. Well, alone with Mum. And I've woken her up hundreds of times before. I don't know why it feels different this time.

I knock more loudly and turn the door handle. 'Mum? Mu-um, time to be getting ...'

I stop. I look around the big bedroom with its super-king-sized bed.

There's no one here. I'm not even sure the bed has been slept in. It looks as though someone might have lain down on top of the white covers and the multiple lacy white pillows.

'Mum?' I check the en suite bathroom I've envied so often, even the walk-in wardrobe. All empty. 'Mum!'

Where on earth can she be? Usually if Mum isn't lying on the chaise longue in the conservatory or the settee in the sitting room, she's in her room. And now, at ten in the morning, when she's due to go and see a doctor in an hour, she's disappeared completely.

The house seemed too big and empty last night. What if Mum hadn't been here even then? The room seems to echo around me, cold, almost threatening. I run downstairs and check every room, then go out into the back garden, but I know she won't be there. I could see most of it from her bedroom, but I check the far corners just to be sure. It's as empty as the house.

I check Corinne and Jonathan's old rooms, just for something to do, but there's no one there.

What should I do? Where can I look? Who should I phone?

I feel dizzy with confusion and a lurking fear. I'm not sure I can reach Dad, and what help would he be in any case? There's no one I can turn to nearby. Mum doesn't have any close friends. It has to be Corinne, although even she is too far away.

I call her mobile.

'Lily? I'm in a meeting just now.'

'This is urgent. Mum's disappeared.'

'What? Okay, excuse me, just a moment.' There are muffled sounds while she presumably exits the meeting. 'Okay, I can talk to you now. Tell me what's happened.'

I do the best as I can, working hard to keep my voice from wobbling.

'Have you tried her mobile?'

'Corinne, Mum never uses her mobile.' But just to be sure, I run up the wide staircase and enter her bedroom again. There it is, the phone Dad insisted she have, sitting on her bedside table. 'It's still here,' I say dully.

'Right, we need to think straight. Has she taken her handbag? Anything else?'

I wonder why I hadn't thought to check those things. I'm obviously useless in a crisis. I check now and say, 'She might have taken a handbag, although she has loads so I can't be sure … Nothing else seems to have gone.'

'Maybe she's just gone to the doctor's early, on her own?' Even to my ears Corinne's voice doesn't sound hopeful.

'Maybe,' I say.

'Right, this is what you're going to do. Head down to the GP surgery yourself, see if she's there, and if not you'd better explain she'll be late for the appointment. Phone me again after that. Then you can start walking around town, see if you can find her.'

'She never just walks around town.'

'I know. But she never just disappears, either.'

I try to supress a shiver. 'Right, I'm heading out now. I'll be in touch.'

Mum isn't at the doctor's surgery and she isn't anywhere around town that I can see. I look in all the shops, even the coffee shops she hates, but there's no sign of her. I wish she had a friend in the town she might have popped in to see, but she doesn't. When I was younger she'd been on good terms with the parents of some of Jonathan and Corinne's friends, and she would always chat politely when she met Gemma's mum, but she never sought them out and gradually people stopped inviting her places. There were the grander families she entertained when Dad was home, but none of them lived in the town. I can't think of any reason she would have gone to them now.

I phone Heather, as a last resort. Maybe Mum had mentioned something to her, about an outing. Anything. But she hasn't. I try to keep my tone light, so she doesn't realise how worried I am. I know Mum would be mortified if she thought there was a fuss.

So that just leaves the paths by the water.

I shiver as I head down there, although it's another warm and sunny day.

For no particular reason, I head upstream first, past the harbour and under the ugly concrete bridge that takes tourists to the beaches of Borra. After that the path peters out, and when there's no sign of her (I even ask a passing dog walker who looks blank), I turn back and walk the other way, towards the dangerous expanse of mudflats, and the sea.

Corinne is driving down, and she must have phoned Jonathan because he calls me as I reach the turn in the path beyond the sailing club, where the town is suddenly hidden and all you can see are the flat green meadows, low brown mudbanks, and grey-blue sea.

'Lily, tell me what's happened.'

I tell him as much as I can.

'I should have come home more often,' he says, surprisingly. Jonathan isn't given to self-criticism. 'But my shifts have been horrendous and with working towards my membership ...'

He pauses, as though waiting for me to say his excuses for him. Instead I'm thinking about all the things *I* should have done: stayed home more, talked to Mum, involved her. I was the one close at hand, who had the chance to help. The two trips to Kirkdouglas are the only things I've done with her the entire summer, despite all my resolutions.

He says, 'I can finish here after lunch. I'll drive up then.'

'Okay.'

'Dad's on his way home too.'

That makes me feel even worse. Jonathan and Corinne coming home like this is unheard of; Dad interrupting his business dealings means they think something's very wrong indeed.

But right now there's just me.

I begin to walk more quickly along the barren coastal path. I haven't seen anything to suggest that Mum might have been here, but somehow I feel that she has. This is the path she used to like walking. I begin to jog, to get to her as soon as possible.

It's crazy and unreasonable. She could be anywhere. And there's no real danger here, nothing to worry about as long as you don't go out on the flats. I start to run harder. What if she has gone out there?

I round another headland to where the dunes begin to rise into low cliffs and the wide area of the mudflats is exposed by the retreating tide. I look out across the deceptively smooth, brown expanse. And then I see her.

At least, I see *something*. There's a figure lying on the ground, motionless. I think it's Mum. She's on the shore, not out on the flats.

I begin to run even faster. I'm too far away to be able to recognise her, but somehow I know. She's here. I've found her. And she's completely still.

I run so fast my breath is coming in great gasps. The figure doesn't move as I pound up beside it, doesn't respond when I yell, 'Mum? Mum!'

I shudder to a stop and kneel down beside her. She's ice cold. How long has she been here? Is she …?

Then she opens her eyes and looks at me, saying nothing, and closes them again, as though by doing that she can shut me out.

I sink down onto the ground beside her, trying to catch my breath. 'Mum! Mum, you're here. You're all right. I was ... worried.'

She still says nothing and I begin to rub her hands, trying to revive her. She's so still and cold I start to think about hypothermia, even if I don't really know what the symptoms are.

'Mum, are you okay? You need to move. You can't just lie here.' I take off my fleece and try, clumsily, to wrap it around her.

She says, without opening her eyes, 'I just wanted to be somewhere quiet.'

'You've missed your doctor's appointment, Mum.'

She says nothing.

Now I've found her, and she's all right, or at least unharmed, I can feel anger rising within me.

'We were worried about you! Corinne and Jonathan are both on their way home. Mum! We were worried sick. You can't do this.'

She gives a very slight shrug of her shoulders. After another long pause she says, 'I'm all right. Just give me a while ...'

I phone Corinne and Jonathan to tell them I've found her. Corinne begins to cry, so I know she'd feared the worst too.

'Try and get her back to the house, I'll be there in

under an hour,' she says, sniffing.

'Come on, let's go home,' I say to Mum. 'Corinne will be back soon.' I take her hand and give it a little tug. 'Mum?'

'I think I'll stay here for a while longer.' Still in the same dull, muted voice.

'You can't, Mum. You're freezing. The ground's wet and muddy.' How can this possibly be my pristine mother, lying among the tide-washed debris? 'How long have you been here?'

She doesn't answer. I'm not sure she's even listening. 'Mum! Come on! You've got to get up.'

'Give me a minute.'

'That's what you always say!' I suddenly snap. Usually her slow vagueness irritates me, but now I'm infuriated. Or desperate. 'Why are you always so – so passive? So *nothing*? Mum, you've got to move! You can't stay here.'

'Your father is away,' she says. I don't know if that is excuse or explanation.

'I know that, but he's worried about you too. He's on his way home. We're all worried about you, Mum. We want you to get … better.' Still nothing. 'Mum, you haven't – you haven't taken anything, have you?'

Mum opens her eyes then and looks at me as though I'm a very long way away. 'Why would I take something? I'm not ill.' She swallows and takes a shallow breath. 'I'm not ill. Am I?'

'You're going to be fine,' I say.

She doesn't say any more, but she does push herself into a sitting position and I help her, so relieved she's moving I can feel tears in my eyes.

I pull her arms through the sleeves of the fleece as though she's a child. 'I don't know if you're ill, but you're really cold and I think we should go home.'

She glances at me and then away, the greying hair falling across her face. Why hadn't I realised how wrong things were, when she hasn't even kept her hair nicely tinted?

I take her arm and help her to her feet. She's started to shiver, and I'm frantic to get her back home. What if she collapses? I can't carry her. Should I phone an ambulance?

'Come on Mum,' I say, sniffing back tears. 'Come on, let's see if you can walk.'

She allows me to lead her over the shingle and back to the path. It seems to take forever, but at least we're moving.

'Don't cry, Lily. You were never the kind of little girl who cried.' And then, so faintly I hardly hear, 'I'm so sorry.'

'I'm not crying,' I say, shaking my hair from my eyes. She doesn't look at me, so she doesn't see that with my other hand I'm wiping away the stupid tears threatening to fall.

Tom

I phone Lily late on Monday afternoon. I'm feeling good. The training session went well – although Lily didn't turn up at all. After lunch Sarah and I went for a walk and she made it all the way to the local park. She's still up and about, helping Mum in the kitchen, not washed out by the effort.

'Hey, how's it going?' I say when Lily picks up. I've got an idea for us to do something together this evening. She isn't the only one who can make plans.

'Tom, this isn't a good time.'

'What? Are you okay?'

'Yes, I'm fine. Look, I'll call you later, okay?'

And she ends the call just like that.

So much for being interested in me, for us starting to get on so well. Why would she brush me off just like that? I'm surprised and hurt – and a bit pissed off. Then, when I've calmed down and thought it through, I wonder if she hadn't sounded upset rather than cross. Maybe she isn't okay, despite what she said. Maybe that's why she didn't come to the sailing club this morning.

I message Gemma. *You heard from Lily?*

No. Sent a message and no reply. Just sent another but it hasn't even gone through. Think her phone's switched off. Why?

Just wondered. Night.

It's too late to do anything tonight, especially if she's switched her phone off. I check and she isn't online, as far as I can see. That makes me more worried than ever. I don't think Lily normally switches off her mobile. If she has now, I'm not so vain as to think it's anything to do with me.

Lily's phone is still switched off in the morning. Gemma comes round to debate it with me.

'Something's wrong,' she says. 'I wonder if she's ill? Or it's something to do with the gala?'

I don't think it's the latter but I'm not sure what else it can be. 'You could phone her on the landline?'

'No. We never use the house phones.' Gemma chews her lip, anxious.

'Why don't you just go round and see her?' Sarah isn't really supposed to be in on the conversation, but she's here anyway. 'That's what I would do.'

'I suppose I could,' says Gemma doubtfully. 'Although we normally arrange things in advance.'

'Come on, we'll go together.' I stand up. We might as well go right now. I feel restless and uneasy.

When we turn the corner onto the poshest street in the old town, where Lily's house holds pride of place, Gemma comes to a stop.

'Something is wrong,' she says.

'How do you know?' It all looks the same to me: pretty, painted houses, cars lining the narrow road.

'That's Lily's sister Corrine's car. And I'm not completely sure, but I think that sporty one there is her brother's. They hardly ever both come home, except for Christmas.'

'Lily has an older brother?'

'Yes. He's a doctor somewhere down south.' Gemma shrugs that off as irrelevant, although I'm wondering just how much I don't know about Lily Hildebrand. 'Maybe we should go away, I don't want to disturb them.'

'No way,' I say. 'I want to know what's going on.'

I carry on along the narrow pavement, Gemma reluctantly in my wake. We turn through the wrought iron gates and up the wide stone steps. Lily's house is the only one on the street with a paved yard. There are no flowers in it but two trees that look like they're something special.

I ring the bell, Gemma standing slightly behind me.

It's just occurred to me that I've never met Lily's family. Is she ashamed of me and wanting to keep me away? Now it's me who's thinking maybe we shouldn't have come after all, but it's too late to turn back.

The door is opened by a tall, slim man of around thirty, with neat, dark hair and an irritated expression. 'Yes? Oh, hi Gemma. It is Gemma, isn't it?'

'Yes.'

'How can I help?'

'We came to see Lily,' I say, when Gemma doesn't reply. I would have thought that's obvious.

Instead of nodding and inviting us in, he frowns. 'Ah. Well. We're a bit preoccupied just now.'

'Is everything all right?' For once Gemma asks the right question. It's better coming from her than me; the man is looking down his nose at me as though he doesn't like what he sees.

Now he turns to Gemma, who's still standing slightly back from the door. 'Yes. Well, no, not quite.' He pauses and seems to realise he needs to give some explanation. 'Our mother is ... a little unwell. We're waiting for a nurse to arrive.' He looks up and down the street, as though she might materialise at any time.

'I see,' says Gemma. 'Well, maybe this isn't a good time ...'

'I'll tell Lily you called,' he says in a tone of dismissal.

As we go back across the little courtyard Gemma looks up. I follow her gaze and think I see someone move back from an upstairs window.

I don't ask but I guess that's Lily's bedroom.

So she really doesn't want to see us.

'Do you think it's serious?' says Gemma. 'Lily's mum?'

I shrug. I really don't know. Surely if it's serious she'd be in hospital? But then, if it's nothing much, why are all the family home? And why is Lily, who takes absolutely everything in her stride, hiding away?

'Maybe she just doesn't want to talk to us,' I say – whether to Gemma or myself, I don't know.

Lily

I watch Gemma and Tom leave. They don't make any big push to come in, and anyway I don't want to see them. Normally I'm fine, I just keep busy and deal with whatever life throws at me. But I don't feel capable of either of those things right now.

Jonathan comes back into Mum's bedroom where we've gathered, waiting for the community psychiatric nurse to arrive. The GP came out to see her yesterday afternoon and he's arranged this. Mum is lying on the bed and although none of us say why, we aren't keen to leave her alone.

'Gemma and some boy,' Jonathan says to me.

'Yeah, I saw.'

'I didn't think you'd want them to come in just now.'

'No.' I shake my head.

'A new boyfriend?' says Corinne, trying to sound chatty.

'No. Just a friend.' I don't have time or energy for

a boyfriend just now. If I hadn't got so distracted by Tom and the gala and everything, maybe Mum would be okay.

Jonathan says he'll stay with Mum. I think he's concerned that having all three of us there is worrying her. Not that she looks worried. Mostly she either dozes or stares at the ceiling.

'What do you think's wrong?' I say to Corinne once we get downstairs. We'd talked about things a bit yesterday but I don't seem to have taken anything in. 'Why is she like this?'

We go into the kitchen and Corinne automatically reaches for the kettle, but it feels like she's doing it to delay answering. Eventually she says, 'She's depressed.' She lets out a long breath. 'I mean, not just unhappy but seriously depressed. It's not the first time.'

'It's not?' I stare at her. I'd slumped on one of the kitchen chairs, but now I sit upright. 'What do you mean? When has it happened before?' And how come I didn't know?

'I thought you knew. She had a spell like this after you were born, you won't remember that of course, and then another a few years later.'

'No, I didn't know.' I'm angry now. There's something wrong with my mum and no one has even thought to tell me? Corinne made that vague request for me to do more with her, Dad asked me to see she went to the doctor's, but no one told me it could be serious – *had been* serious before?

'You were only little at the time, and then I suppose we thought she'd got better. It's not really something you want to talk about, is it? Mental illness?' She speaks calmly, but I can tell she's uncomfortable because she won't meet my eye.

'But what's wrong with her?'

She shifts uncomfortably. 'I think the first time they said it was postnatal depression. The second time, I suppose it was just depression. She was in hospital for a while that time. Do you really not remember?'

I think back, trying really hard, but I can't come up with anything. I was always busy as a child, same as now I suppose. Does that mean I don't even notice when something important happens? What's wrong with me?

Corinne finishes making the coffee and we sit there in silence. I don't know what to do, and if I did I don't know if I've got the energy to do it. I hate this. Hate hate hate it.

Tom

Lily doesn't come to the training session at the sailing club on Thursday. John Forsyth says she phoned to give her apologies, and really we don't need her anymore. Now they've been here a few times, the kids know what they're doing and the parents have stopped hanging around and needing attention.

The kids are a good bunch. I think we'll get some reasonable novices' races out of them. The fact that there is so much activity down at the club seems to have brought out more of the experienced sailors, too, which has increased the entries for some of the proper races. John Forsyth is pleased with himself, talking about hanging out the bunting and ordering new starting and finishing flags.

The regatta is going to be a success, just as Lily envisaged.

I send her a message to tell her so and she replies *Great! I knew it would be.*

It's the first contact I've had with her for two days. It isn't much, but it's better than nothing. I hope she'll be back in circulation soon. Life is kind of dull without her. I might complain about the regatta stuff taking up my spare time, but I don't really mind when Lily is around. Now it isn't nearly as much fun.

In the afternoon, Sarah has arranged for Gemma and me to practise a song we're supposed to be doing for the talent show. It was Sarah's idea that we should enter, because she'd seen online that they needed more competitors. Gemma refused to enter on her own, so guess who got landed with the guitar accompaniment? Maybe now Sarah is doing so much better I should stop giving in to her so easily.

'You know, I think I should be your manager,' she says, sitting cross-legged on the settee, in shorts and a T-shirt. She looks fine. I wonder if she's even put on a tiny bit of weight. I'm so pleased I decide to carry on humouring her for a bit longer. 'You're pretty good, or you would be if you practised more.'

Well, maybe not that much longer. 'We've already played it through about twenty times!'

'And you need to extend your repertoire.'

'I'm only performing one song!' says Gemma.

'Absolutely,' I agree. The Burns song she's chosen is apparently one of the more simple ones, but it still stretches my skills to the limit.

'You need at least one more, in case you get through to the final,' says Sarah firmly. 'The best four go through to a final round and have to do a second performance. You can't perform the same thing twice.'

'Why not?' I say. 'And anyway, who says we'll get through that far?'

'I do. I told you, Gemma's voice is amazing.'

'I'm still not sure I want to enter,' says Gemma, pulling round the end of her ponytail so she can chew on it.

'I've already sent in the form,' Sarah says smugly. 'Mum lent me the entry money. So you can't back out now.'

Gemma's pale, freckled face takes on a greenish tinge. She isn't going to try and back out, is she? When Sarah is having so much fun and I've got the guitar re-strung *and* learnt the chords?

'We'll just have to do our best,' I say quickly. 'And if we have to learn a second piece, can we make it a short one? You should choose, Gem, I haven't a clue about this kind of music.'

Fortunately that distracts her. 'Yes, a short one. That's a good idea.'

And later, when I'm mulling over how flat life is without Lily around, I have another good idea.

Gemma's still in our house, showing Sarah how to make a super smoothie. Sarah is chatting away to her and looking happy and carefree.

She thrusts a glass of something thick and fluorescent orange into my hand. 'Try it! It's carrot and apricot.'

'Er ...'

'Go on. It's amazing. And so good for you.'

I take a cautious sip. 'That's actually okay. But no, I don't want any more!' I put my hand over the top of the glass. There is only so much fresh fruit and veg you can take at one time. 'Save some for Mum and Dad.'

'Oh yes. Good thinking.'

'Yeah. And I've been thinking about something else.' I turn to Gemma. 'Didn't you say you and Lily had talked about organising a beach barbecue?'

'Ye-es. But Lily's still not doing much ...'

'What I was thinking was, why don't we organise it – you and me? We don't have to rely on Lily for everything. If we aim for, I don't know, the middle of next week, hopefully things will be better at home for Lily and she'll be able to come along.' I like the idea of doing something for Lily for a change.

Gemma looks doubtful, licking orange stuff off her fingers. 'I'm not sure. We don't know who Lily was planning to invite.'

'We can make our own list. It's not exactly difficult, is it? We should go to Borra. We won't be short of space there, and people can bring their own food and stuff.'

'I think it's a brilliant idea!' says Sarah.

'You can't come,' I say immediately.

'Why not? I'm loads better.' She looks mutinous.

'Sarah, it'll go on til late. There'll be alcohol. Do you really think Mum and Dad would let you come? You're too young.'

'Oh,' she says. And actually she looks pleased to be stopped from coming for a reason other than her health. 'But I can still help making the arrangements. Can't I?'

'Sounds good to me,' says Gemma, giving me a nod that Sarah can't see.

'Yes, all help appreciated,' I say. Gemma's clearly thinking it'll be good for Sarah to be involved. And why not? If it helps us, too, it's a win-win.

Lily

Dad and Corinne and Jonathan all stay home the whole week. It's like there's been a death in the family. We're all pussy-footing around the place, talking in lowered voices. The CPN (I know all the terminology now) has been to see Mum and she's on some kind of medication but we've been told it'll take at least a fortnight for it to start working.

Mum does seem a little better, at least enough to be embarrassed about all the fuss she's caused. But then, she does always try harder when Dad or Corinne or Jonathan are in the house.

She's up and dressed by mid-morning, and she eats the meals that Corinne cooks. Corinne makes cooking seem really simple so I decide I'll carry on when she leaves. Maybe I can ask Mum for advice, and that will get her involved? I'm really worried about how things will be when it's just Mum and me. I don't know what I'll do if she goes back to being like she was before.

Nobody has said how long they're staying home, but I know it won't be for long. And true enough, on Saturday evening after we've all eaten together like a proper family, they start announcing their plans for getting away.

Mum has gone to bed. Before the rest of us can disperse Dad says, 'We need to talk.'

Jonathan gets in quickly, as though he knows what's coming, 'I have to head back to Manchester tomorrow.'

'And I really need to be in Edinburgh on Monday, although I could go up first thing in the morning if that would help.' Corinne looks at Dad as she speaks.

My stomach clenches. Are they going to go away and leave me? So far all Mum's done is lie for god knows how long on a cold, wet beach, but what about next time? Am I supposed to keep an eye on her twenty-four hours a day? Stop her if she tries …

I abandon the thought halfway.

'I'm supposed to be in London on Wednesday,' says Dad, looking unusually uncomfortable under the stares of my older siblings. 'I was hoping that by then …'

'I don't think Lily should be left here to cope with Mum on her own,' says Jonathan. He's never been one to hold back his opinions, but it isn't often they chime so completely with mine. 'She's too young for all the responsibility. She already has more freedom than she should.' Okay, maybe they don't completely chime with mine.

Corinne says, 'Lily's done brilliantly, but I think all of us have taken it for granted that she'd be here and look after things.' I haven't done brilliantly, but I do appreciate her support. She pats my hand and says, looking at Dad, 'So we shouldn't leave her at home alone with Mum so much. And definitely not at all right now.'

Dad sighs. 'I suppose I could get someone to deputise for me,' he says reluctantly. 'I could stay home this coming week and we can see how it goes.'

'Things aren't going to improve in a week,' says Jonathan, in what I think of as his I'm-a-doctor-I-know-best voice. 'It's going to take a while. You can't make any predictions at this stage.'

'But she will get better,' I say, looking around at them all. 'Won't she? You said this has happened before, and she got better.'

'I think this depression is more serious than last time,' says Jonathan. 'And it's been allowed to progress untreated far longer.'

It's like he's trying to make me feel guilty, despite what Corinne just said – which he doesn't have to do, because I already feel it. I want to say, *I didn't know! No one told me I was supposed to be looking out for Mum.* But the truth is, I hadn't *wanted* to look out for her. I'd ignored her because that was the easiest way. Now as I look back, it's obvious that something was wrong. But I'd just carried on with my own life and pretended it wasn't happening, kept busy. Maybe I'd made sure I was even busier than normal, so I didn't need to see.

I hunch down, pulling my cardigan around my shoulders. I feel like I'm ill too, shivery and a bit detached from reality. I don't want this to be reality.

Dad sighs again. 'Okay, then. I suppose we have to deal with the situation we find ourselves in.' He sounds like he's chairing a business meeting. 'Take stock and then move forward.' He pauses and looks around, as though he still hopes one of us will offer to take everything in hand. When we don't, he reaches for his phone and starts looking through his calendar. 'I suppose, if I have to, I can rearrange things and stay home until at least the middle of the week after next.'

He looks at Corinne and she pulls a face but says, 'I'll need to check with my boss but I might be able to get a couple of days off then.'

'Right, so that's a fortnight covered. We'll review things after that. The CPN is coming in every other day, I understand. It's not as if your mother won't have support.'

I know I should say something like, *And I'll be here, too. I can help.* But I don't.

For the first time in my life I'm in a situation that I don't feel capable of controlling. I have completely and absolutely no idea what to do.

Tom

The preparations for the barbecue are going well. Sarah is definitely useful. She takes the lists of people Gemma and I have made and sends invites using our phones. She even collates the responses! It's like having a secretary, but she enjoys it and it's not the kind of thing that's going to tire her out. Plus it saves me having to do it.

Lily seems impressed with what we've done, too. I see her briefly at the sailing club on Monday and fill her in. She's surprised, a bit distracted, but seems pleased. I ask if everything is okay at home and she says it is. I don't believe her.

We'd decided on Wednesday for the barbecue, on the beach at Borra, and I just hope she'll be there or the whole thing will have been a total waste of time.

And she is! She messages to ask whether she can get a lift out, and what she should bring. Her messages sound a little subdued, but at least she's coming.

Gemma's brother Liam drives the three of us out there. My dad says he'll give us a lift back and we should phone to tell him when, but not to make it too late. It'll be so good when we can drive ourselves. I need to take learning more seriously.

Lily is quiet as we cart the baskets and cool boxes along the narrow paths through the gorse down to the sand. People are handing out beers and ciders. Gemma goes off with Molly Douglas and Sally-Anne to arrange where we should set up the barbecues. I thought she might have stuck with me and Lily, until I remember Sally-Anne is Jamie's cousin. We can't compete with that.

Lily nods to one or two people, makes a few comments, but even that seems like an effort. She spreads out one of those expensive double-sided picnic blankets and collapses onto it.

'At least it's not raining,' she sighs. 'It might later.'

Nice that she's so cheerful.

'Yeah, let's look on the bright side. It's fairly warm, and more than five people have turned up.'

'Is that the bright side?' She gives a very faint smile.

'Sure. Barbecues in Scotland are always risky.'

'I suppose.'

I don't know why she's so unenthusiastic. The barbecue was originally her idea. She checks her phone, as though hoping for something, and then gives the broadest smile I'd seen since we picked her up.

'What?'

'Donny's agreed to my suggestion.'

'What suggestion?'

'You know he was struggling to find somewhere for his Gala Parade applicants to get together for a practice run? Anywhere in town they're bound to be seen and then the old people will start objecting. So we thought – why not get them to come out here?'

I'm not exactly delighted. Gemma and I (and Sarah) have done all the organising for this barbecue, and she's hijacking it for something completely different.

She senses I'm not keen. 'What? You've got a problem with that?'

I sigh. I can't change it now. 'I suppose not.'

'They should be here soon. Come on, let's walk up to the road and look out for their cars.' Lily holds out her hand.

We walk back up the narrow path, the thorns of the gorse scraping at our bare legs. Lily seems to have woken up now.

Donny's older brother Karl appears driving an old mini whose engine definitely doesn't sound healthy. A few people get out of it. Karl shakes his head when Donny invites him to stay, and turns to head back to town. Behind them, six or seven people climb out of the kind of campervan you see in hippy road movies. One man has a kaftan on and long hair and a beard. Another two people, equally tall, are wearing long dresses and full make-up, possibly going for the gala queen look. The rest are in ordinary clothes which makes those three stand out all the more.

Lily seems delighted, chatting to Donny, getting him to introduce us, and then leading everyone back to the shore. I'm a bit worried about what kind of reception we'll get down there. I don't recognise many of Donny's friends and this is supposed to be a barbecue for our school year plus a few of the year below, not just anyone who wants to turn up.

I needn't have worried. Donny and Lily's excitement is infectious. They round up Sally-Anne so she can tell us the route of the procession, then they get everyone to clear an area of the sand so the new arrivals can strut their stuff.

'There might be a few more on the day,' says Donny happily. He's wearing a court jester's costume and seems to be in his element.

Not everyone is as enthused by the whole thing as Donny. Most of them have some kind of rainbow colours on their clothes, but not all are keen on being in the spotlight. There's a girl, Jo, from the year above us at school, who's looking anywhere but at people, like if she doesn't acknowledge us then we won't know she's there.

Donny's worked out a dance manoeuvre, a kind of Monster Mash but trying to move forward at the same time. As I watch I realise I do actually know a few more of the people. They're from the town, but don't normally draw much attention to themselves. One man sees me staring and looks away, self-consciously. Donny makes this whole thing look easy, he's a natural performer, but some of the others are definitely stepping out of their comfort zone.

'Okay, one more try,' he says, shaking his ribboned stick so that the bells on the end ring tinnily. 'We've got to keep moving with the parade. We want the maximum amount of people to see us.'

They go through their routine again. Everyone seems to be getting into it now, even Jo. It's hard not to join in the laughter, with Donny doing his moves.

As they finish, Lily turns to the audience, 'And remember, you lot, no word of this to anyone. We want it to be a surprise.'

'It'll be a surprise all right,' murmurs Gemma.

Donny's friends are fun but I'm glad when the practice run ends. Donny walks back up to the campervan with them, saying he's going to change out of his outfit – 'It's a little tight in places!' Then he'll come back down and join us again.

Lily says, 'Donny's cool. It's really great what he's doing.'

'It is,' I say. I mean it, but I can't help adding, 'I wonder what his parents think of, you know, all his antics.'

'They seem happy enough.' She sighs. 'They're so supportive. They're at all his performances and everything.'

'And your parents aren't supportive?' I think of the big house, all the gadgets, never short of money …

Her expression closes down. 'Not in the same way.'

She's changed since whatever happened last week. Previously she might have been annoying, but she was always completely straightforward. She wanted to hold your hand, she held it. She wanted to kiss you, she kissed you. Now she swings from friendly to distant in seconds, and I can't work her out at all.

'How is your mum?'

'Fine.' If it's possible, her face looks even more shuttered. I try not to be hurt. It's her business. If anyone knows that family business is private it should be me.

She goes over to the people standing near the barbecue. I leave her to it and wander down to where the waves lap the rough sand. Looking west, the water is slate grey, a sign of storms to come; but just now the wind is soft and warm and the sky almost blue. It's good that there isn't more wind or I might wish I were out there sailing. I'd really much rather be somewhere on my own than at a stupid party like this. But organising it was my idea, and if you're going to have a beach barbecue, you can't get a much better evening than this for it. Loads of people have turned up. Lily seems happy now she's talking to them and not me. So why aren't I having a bloody good time, like everyone else?

I skim a couple of stones into the waves, but I'm even rubbish at that, so I go back and crack open a beer. I chat to people occasionally and watch Lily swanning from group to group. This is how it always is for me at parties, an outsider, someone looking in. Previously I haven't minded.

Lily comes to find me much later on, as the light is fading to dusk. I guess she's had a fair amount to drink herself. She's moving in that loose-limbed way of the mildly intoxicated, swinging one of those disgusting sickly sweet ciders from one hand.

'Tom. Thomas. You and Gemma did a good thing, organising this.' She plonks herself down on the grass beside me. The beach here is shale rather than nice fine sand, so once the barbecue was finished we moved the party further up onto the grass. Far more comfortable.

'Yeah,' I say. 'You're not the only one who can organise things. Amazing, isn't it?'

'That's not what I meant.' She looks hurt.

I say quickly, 'It's all going well. Everyone's having fun.'

'Aye. Tha's good.' Maybe Lily is more than mildly intoxicated. I've never seen her not in control and it doesn't seem right.

She suddenly rises to her feet, staggering slightly, and puts out her hand to me. 'Come on, let's go somewhere else.'

I let her pull me up and follow her through the gorse and rocks. I grab a couple of cans of coke to take with us. The last thing she needs is more alcohol.

When we reach a place where towering grey boulders form a private alcove she takes my hand again and pulls me down to sit beside her.

'This is nice and private,' she says, tossing aside the empty cider bottle and putting both arms around me.

I pull back. 'Are you embarrassed to be seen kissing me? Is that why we've come here?' I've been watching her from a distance all evening, but I'm not going to be at her beck and call.

'Not 'barrassed. Prefer private.'

She touches her lips to mine and then withdraws so that she can look me directly in the eyes. 'And it's not just kissing I'm thinking about.'

Jesus! Where did that come from? I jolt upright. I can feel my heart, and something else, quiver. It isn't as though I haven't thought about sex with Lily. Gorgeous, curvy, adventurous Lily. But not now, not like this.

'Lily, you've had way too much to drink.'

'No I haven't. Not nearly enough. Come on Tom.' She leans in again and kisses me, such delicate little kisses that I give way for a while and kiss her back. But soon we're lying down, and the kisses are getting totally heated, and she has her hands under my T-shirt.

I roll away. 'Lily, for godsake. This isn't a good idea.'

'What? You don't want me?'

'It's not about what I want,' I say, turning away and adjusting my jeans. I feel kind of high and shaky, and it isn't from the alcohol.

'So? Are you scared? Is that it?'

That makes me look back at her, and not be distracted by the wide eyes and soft red lips. 'No, I'm not scared.' What can I say that doesn't sound totally trite? Because I respect you too much for a quick roll in the sand? Because you're drunk and you'll regret it in the morning?

'You are,' she says, this time with a sneer.

'Piss off, Lily. I just know there's something wrong. You're upset, otherwise you wouldn't be acting like this.'

'I am not upset!' she shouts. 'What have I got to be upset about?'

I shrug, because I don't really know. 'You're angry. You're using me to distract yourself.'

'Don't you dare take that superior tone with me. I'm perfectly fine! F. I. N–' A strange sound cuts her off. It takes a second to realise it came from her. Is she ... is she *crying*?

'Of course you are,' I soothe. 'Let's just sit here for a while, maybe drink these cokes. And if you want to talk about anything ...'

I offer her a can but she bats it away, blinking furiously. 'Why would I want to talk? If you don't like me, just say so. Don't make pathetic excuses.' She spits the words out.

'Look, Lily.' I put out a hand, trying to be calming. I wish I knew what was going on. 'What I mean is ...' I try to think of something to say, to make everything better. Before I've come up with any words she's jumped to her feet.

'Thanks for nothing,' she says and strides off back towards the noise of the party.

Now not only is she drunk and upset, but she's completely furious with me too.

I stay where I am for a while. I'm a bit stunned by what just happened, plus my head is spinning from the beers I've drunk. And from the kissing. I crack open a can of soft drink and swallow some down, but it doesn't make me feel any better. I can't stay here, though. I really don't know what Lily will do next. And whatever her problems are, they're obviously not the sort to be solved by a fun evening at the beach.

Lily

I wake up with a killer headache and all too clear a memory of what happened the night before.

My god, how could I be so stupid stupid stupid?

And how could bloody Tom Owen turn me down like that!

The headache diminishes after two mugs of extra-strong coffee, but the embarrassment remains.

I acted like a total fool. I have no idea what I was thinking. Probably I hadn't been thinking at all. It'd been such a relief to get out of the house, away from Mum doing nothing and Dad trying and failing to be patient with her. It was the first time I'd gone out properly since finding Mum. I'd been really chuffed, like Tom and Gemma had organised the whole barbecue just for me. And Donny and his crowd turning up had been the cherry on the cake. I'd shown off, wanting to take credit for them being there. But then most of them had left and I'd started to lose that happy feeling. So I'd taken the various drinks people had passed me and swallowed them down far too quickly and then …

Oh god, I *really* don't want to think of the look of distaste in Tom's eyes when he pulled away from me. Am I really that disgusting?

I don't know how I'm ever going to live this down. But as sitting moping never helped anyone, I make an enormous cooked breakfast (it may not be healthy but I remember Corinne saying it helps with a hangover) and insist that Mum gets dressed and comes downstairs to eat with Dad and me. This is one meal I can cook without needing a recipe book.

Gemma comes round later. She's desperate for information.

'Whatever happened with you and Tom?' she says, coming straight to the point. At least we're out in the garden so no one can overhear us. If my parents are even interested.

'Nothing.'

'I thought you were getting on really well. Then on the way back in the car you wouldn't even look at each other, never mind speak.'

'I had too much to drink, that's all,' I say.

'Yes. And that normally makes you more chatty, not less.'

'I felt sick,' I say flatly. And I did, but it wasn't because of the alcohol. 'Anyway, what did you think of Donny's crowd for the parade? A bit different, hey?'

Gemma narrows her eyes. 'I'm still not sure this is a good idea. The committee are going to go into meltdown when they see it.'

'So?'

'I wish we'd never got involved in the whole gala thing.' She sighs.

I'm not having that. Even if I haven't got much time to be involved myself right now, I'm not going to let all our work go to waste. 'It's going to be brilliant. Think how well the regatta preps are going. And you're entering the talent show. Come on Gem, how can you not be looking forward to that?'

'You mean how could I possibly look forward to it?'

'You're a brilliant singer.' I'm starting to feel better, telling someone what to do.

'No I'm not. I'm just okay. And I hate singing in public.'

'Well if you're just okay, I don't know what I am,' I say, trying to rally her. I'm determined she's going to enter the talent show. 'Have you decided what you're going to perform?'

To my surprise she nods, although not with any enthusiasm. 'I'm doing a Rabbie Burns song. Nice and safe. What about you?' she says, turning the question back on me. 'You really need to do something, too. Apparently the number of entries is still low. If I have to sing the least you can do is take part as well.'

'Maybe I will,' I say. I'm not bothered either way. Making a fool of myself there can't be as bad as what happened last night.

'You're definitely doing it,' she says. 'I'll put your entry in. Sarah put in one for me without even asking.'

'Good for her.'

'At least I won't be alone on stage.'

'Who've you got to accompany you?' I'm relieved she hasn't asked me to do it. My piano playing was never great and is now extremely rusty.

'Tom. He's going to play guitar.'

'Oh.' I didn't even know Tom played guitar. I turn away. 'That's good of him.'

'It is. He isn't keen but he's doing it. He's a nice guy, Tom.' She watches me, trying to see my reaction.

I just say, 'Why don't you play piano yourself? You're perfectly capable of playing *and* singing.'

'And be out there all on my own? Are you mad?'

I shake my head. Gemma really needs to get over this fear of performing, but just now I don't have the energy to challenge her on it.

Lily

Unsurprisingly, I don't hear a thing from Tom all day. Dad invites Gemma to have dinner with us, probably because he thinks it will bring Mum out a bit. It certainly helps on the cooking side. Who knew how many ingredients there were in spaghetti bolognaise?

And it makes conversation easier, too, although that's mostly because Dad is cross-questioning Gemma on what she's planning to do with the rest of her life. Mum nods and smiles and says practically nothing. I don't think Gemma even notices anything different. She doesn't ask if I want to talk about things, like Tom did.

After Gemma goes home I do fifty sit-ups and twenty push-ups, because I really can't face going out for a run and I have to do something to prove to myself I'm not completely useless. Then I check my phone for the hundredth time. Nothing. I collapse on my bed and glare at the ceiling.

Mum and Dad are still downstairs. I can hear the television on and the occasional mumble of their voices. That's good, but it's not them I'm worried about right now.

It looks like I'm going to have to take the initiative, if I ever want to see Tom Owen again. Which I do.

Right. Should I phone him, or message? I spend ages trying to decide, which puts me in an even worse mood. I hate indecision.

Eventually I send a message: *You awake?* He should be. It's only eleven.

The answer comes gratifyingly quickly. *I'm awake. And you?*

That makes me smile.

But now I can't think of what else to say, except that I need to see him.

Meet me in the park?

Now?

Fifteen minutes?

I look out of my uncurtained window. It's what passes for dark at this time of year, but the moon is nearly full so it feels more like dusk than night. Not that I'm afraid to go out in the dark – there are streetlights, and Newton St Cuthbert isn't exactly a hotbed of crime.

OK. See you at the bandstand.

Wow, that was quick. Which must be a good sign, mustn't it? I'd half expected him to make some excuse about not being able to get out of the house at this time of night. Either his parents are very easy-going or (more likely) they're already in bed and he's just going to sneak out.

Like I am.

I pull on jeans and a fleece, pick up my trainers and go quietly down the stairs. I open the front door just wide enough to slide through, and I'm away.

I jog a bit on the way to the park, figuring it can count towards one of my runs. I expect to get there before Tom. I definitely live closer. But as I approach the shadowy bandstand I see he's already arrived. A bike is propped up against the railings.

'Hi there,' I say brightly. I'm not going to be all tongue-tied and stupid, no matter how much I feel like it.

'Hi there yourself.' He squints as though he's trying to read my expression. Maybe the park wasn't such a good idea. Somewhere with street lights would have made it easier to see each other. But then other late-night passers-by would be able to see us, and I want privacy.

I decide to get straight in with what I need to say. 'Look, I wanted apologise. About last night. I'd had too much to drink, as you probably realised. I was completely out of order.'

He gives a faint shrug. 'You don't have to apologise.'

'I do. I was behaving like an idiot.'

'You were upset about something.'

I wish he hadn't said that. I'm trying my best to say sorry, something I'm really not good at. Can't he just accept it? I don't need anyone to make excuses for me.

'I'm fine. What do I have to be upset about?'

He moves to sit on the steps of the bandstand, and after a moment I sit down beside him.

He says, 'You think I don't know what it's like to have an illness in the family?'

'I … My mum's not exactly ill.'

'Really?' He tries to look at me again. I hope he can't see much. I feel wrong-footed by the way the conversation is going. He persists. 'So what's wrong?'

'Nothing's wrong.'

He continues in the same quiet voice, 'Then why were all your family home, and why's your dad still there? Your brother said she wasn't well.'

I'd forgotten that he and Gemma called at the house while everyone was home.

'Okay, Mum is a bit … I don't know!' I take a deep breath. He asked, didn't he? And suddenly maybe I do want to talk. 'They say she's depressed, but she's not ill, exactly. I mean, she's not even in bed anymore. She's just kind of vacant and even more infuriating than usual. Why doesn't she just *do* something?' I know I should be sounding sympathetic but it just comes out angry.

'I think when people are depressed, the whole point is that they can't think of anything they *want* to do.'

'But it's so frustrating! She's not physically ill. She has everything in life she could possibly want. I don't understand her.'

'I'm sure she doesn't want to be ill.'

I glare out across the grass at the faint shadows cast by the moon. 'I know you've got illness at home too. But at least Sarah is physically ill. At least there's something definite there.'

'You think so? Really?' Now he turns away and I realise that he's upset, which surprises me. Tom hardly ever seems upset. He says quietly, 'There's been no real diagnosis. They've decided it's Chronic Fatigue Syndrome because they can't pin it down as anything else. And a lot of people think CFS is more a mental than a physical thing.'

'Do they?' That brings me up short. 'But when Sarah was in hospital recently, that was a real illness.'

He laughs, but not as though he's amused. 'Yes, that was real enough. We got lots of sympathy for that one. An ambulance rushing you to hospital? Oh, yes, that scores well on the illness scale.'

'Have people been, what, nasty about Sarah?'

'We know people talk about her behind our backs. And they're not exactly rushing round to spend time with her, are they? She used to have lots of friends her own age, but she never sees them now. They got fed up of her never being able to do things.'

'But she does do things,' I say quickly. Sarah is *so* much better than Mum. 'She did all that art work, and she has ideas, she's interested in stuff.'

'But she hardly goes out, which makes her boring. Apparently.'

'Gemma still sees her,' I say, trying to show things aren't all bad.

'Gemma's nice. She and Sarah get on. And Gemma's not exactly desperate to go out partying every night, is she? She doesn't mind that Sarah has to stay at home.'

'No, Gem wouldn't mind that.' In a way, him getting mad about how things are for Sarah makes me feel better about my family. I know it shouldn't but it does.

'I'm sorry about Sarah,' I offer.

'There's nothing for you to be sorry about. All I'm saying is lots of people have problems, some are just more visible than others. You don't have to pretend they don't exist, either way.'

We're quiet for a moment. This is my opening, and part of me still wants to insist *I don't have any problems*. But he's talked to me about Sarah, which can't have been easy for him. If I take a deep breath and try really hard, maybe I can be honest too.

I don't look at him. 'Well, things aren't great for me, with Mum being like she is.'

He takes my hand and holds it, palm to palm. 'That's what I thought.'

He doesn't ask any more questions and we sit there in the darkness for a while. Then I say, 'She went missing last week. For a whole night. I couldn't find her and I thought ...'

He lets out a long breath. 'Suicide attempt?'

I shake my head in denial. I don't even want to hear the word. 'I don't know! I found her. She was just lying on the mud out by Dundress.' I let the breath go out through my nose, trying to stay calm, swallowing down the lump in my throat. 'I was the only one at home. I couldn't find her.'

'God. That must have been awful.'

'I hadn't even known she was missing! It was only in the morning I realised. If I'd kept a better eye on her–'

'Lily, you're not responsible for your mother.'

'But I was the one at home, wasn't I?' I let go of his hand so I can wave both of mine around. 'There must be something I could have done. Maybe if I was different, liked doing the same kinds of things as she does, maybe that would have helped. You know – if I was a better daughter.' I spit out the words.

'What does she like to do?'

'Well, actually, nothing much.' I give a snort of laughter. 'So I would have had to do nothing, too, just sit around and look pretty. And be bored. But maybe that's what I should have done.'

He takes my hand and says again, 'You're not responsible, Lily. You can't fix everything.'

I really want to argue. Of course I can fix things! That's what I do. But I can feel tears welling in my eyes, because he's being so sympathetic.

I sniff. 'I want things to be like they were.' Mum wasn't always like this. I can remember a time when she did things. 'She used to like cooking.' I wonder if that's why I've made this not-entirely-successful attempt to get in to cooking. 'She was really good at it. And dancing.' I remember when I was at primary school and she taught Gemma and me all sorts of dances – silly ones, difficult ones. 'I think she must have done ballroom dancing at some point.'

'I can't say I know your mum, I've only ever seen her in the distance, but she looks like she would be a good dancer. She's kind of elegant.'

'Yes. I'm not at all like her.'

He nudges me with his knee. 'Hey, this isn't about you, remember?'

I pull a face, even though he won't be able to see it in the dark. 'Do you think I should try and get her to take up dancing again? I wouldn't even know where to start. They don't do ballroom in Newton St Cuthbert, do they?'

'I've no idea. And it's not up to you to do anything, Lily. You don't have to take charge all the time.'

'Hmmph,' I say. I know he's trying to be helpful. 'But I want to make things better.' He doesn't say anything. A thought occurs to me. What if he feels like this about Sarah, but knows there's nothing he can do? I say, 'Mum is taking some kind of medication now, that should help, shouldn't it?'

'Hopefully,' he says, although he doesn't sound convinced. 'Medication isn't always the answer.'

I'm pretty sure now he's talking about his sister. 'Is Sarah taking anything?'

'No. There isn't anything for her to take.'

'But she is getting better, isn't she?'

'Maybe.' He shrugs. 'We've thought she's getting better before.'

I take that in. Years and years of this going on in the family. 'Do you resent all the attention being on Sarah all the time?' I ask quietly. Jonathan and Corinne are phoning home daily now. Corinne makes an effort to chat, but I know they really only want to talk about Mum.

'What? Resent her being ill and me not?'

'Resent all the time it takes up, and the things it stops you doing?' I've never thought before about what it must be like for him, but now it seems obvious – maybe because now it's happening to me. And even then it's in a small way compared to what he's had to deal with. 'Didn't you even swap bedrooms with Sarah, to give her the bigger room? You're the oldest, you should have the best room.'

He doesn't say anything for a long time. Then, very quietly, 'I wish she would get better. For me, as well as for her. We're all selfish really.'

We sit there in silence, and I shift closer to him, because I'm getting cold. 'We can't sit here for ever.'

'No. We can't.' He lets go of my hand and puts his arm around me and we sit for a while longer.

'I should go back,' I say. I've realised I've come out without a key. Dad doesn't always lock the doors but it will be just my luck if he takes it into his head to do so tonight.

'Yeah.' He turns his face to me and brushes back my hair and leans in and touches my lips.

I shift and sink happily into the kiss, a gentle kiss that gradually deepens. It isn't exactly comfortable, sitting side by side on the wooden steps, but we manage surprisingly well.

Eventually he's the one who pulls back. 'Come on, we should go.' At least he sounds regretful. He stands and pulls me to my feet.

'So, only kisses?' I say. I make my tone jokey.

'Only kissing's all right with me,' he says, but he puts his hands on my waist, on my skin beneath my T-shirt, and I give a little shiver. He leans in and kisses me again, and he sighs heavily when we pull apart, so I feel pretty sure that one day kissing won't be all that we're doing.

He walks back to my house with me, wheeling his bike. And would you believe it, Dad *has* actually locked up! Shit. What am I going to do now? My happy mood evaporates. There are no lights on so Dad must have gone to bed. He won't appreciate being woken up. Plus he'll want to know what I've been doing and I don't want to get into discussing that.

'I'll try the conservatory door at the back,' I say, not very hopeful. That, too, is locked.

Tom says, 'You could come back to mine.' His tone is neutral, neither keen nor discouraging.

I consider it. Sneaking in, maybe getting up to Tom's room without being discovered. Spending the night with him, even if we don't actually *do* anything.

I'm tempted. But then, how will I get out again in the morning? I picture the walk of shame.

'No. I've got a better idea. If this stupid scaffolding is here I might as well make use of it. My window's open. If I can just get close enough to climb in ...'

He squints up. 'Do you want me to try first?'

'No I do not! Honestly, do you think girls can't do anything?'

'I was only offering.'

'Well, don't. I'll be fine. You can head back home.'

'You think I'm going to miss the sight of you shimmying up there?'

When he puts it like that, I really wish he wasn't there to watch. I'm not the most graceful of people, and I don't really like heights. But there's no way I'm going to admit that.

I kiss him briefly. 'Goodnight. Okay, here goes.'

It's mortifying. It takes me three goes to get to the first level of the scaffolding (the roofers having inconsiderately removed the lower ladder). And I only manage that when Tom gave me a leg up. So much for being capable and independent.

It gets marginally easier after that. The metal is icy cold against my hands, but comfortingly stable. I scramble up to the next level and then make the mistake of looking down at Tom. He seems an awful long way below.

Instead of offering sympathetic support he whistles softly and says, 'Pity you're not wearing a skirt. Quite a view from here.'

'Bugger off.'

But that distracts me enough to try the next bit. I edge towards my window. The scaffolding has been set up to enable access to the roof, not the house, so there is a scary gap I need to get across. The more I look, the wider it seems to get. But I'm not going to give up now!

So I stop looking and quickly stretch one leg across so my foot is on the window ledge. Okay, halfway. I take a deep breath and swing the other foot over, grasping the top of the window frame with my hands. I've done it! Not very elegantly, maybe, but I'm here.

I pull the window down as far as I can and tumble inside.

I take a few breaths to calm myself and then go back and look out. I feel kind of giggly with relief. 'There. I did it!'

'Well done.' Tom sounds like he's grinning. I hope he's impressed as well as amused.

He raises a hand in farewell, then swings his leg over the bike and cycles off.

I wonder if he realised how terrified I was. Hopefully not. I've admitted one problem tonight, let's not add heights to the mix. I'll just have to remember the key next time – and at least there probably will be a next time. I must be better at apologies than I thought!

Tom

Lily Hildebrand is just as crazy as I'd always thought. The only difference is, I really like her that way. It's an honest, brave kind of crazy. And watching her climb the scaffolding, obviously terrified but still pressing on – that had been both scary and exciting.

I used to deny that she was totally hot because I thought she looked down on all the guys who fancied her. I certainly can't deny it now. After the fiasco on the beach I did think about backing off, calling a break before things got … wherever they were getting. But I know I didn't really want to, and after talking for ages in the dark on the bandstand steps, I want to even less. Weirdly, now that I know her life isn't as perfect as it seems, that Lily has problems like the rest of us, I like her more.

It's about time I take the initiative. In the morning I send her a text: *So how do you feel about dating?*

Specifically or in general?

That makes me smile. *Me. Specifically.* And then I feel completely stupid for asking. Yeah, she likes hanging out with me. But I'm not some kind of high-status boyfriend like bloody Jamie Abernethy. I'm not tall and built and good-looking. Why on earth would she want to date me?

I think I'd quite like that.

I punch the air. Yes!

I make arrangements to see her later at the sailing club. After a moment's hesitation, I go to tell Sarah the news. I have to start somewhere.

She's ecstatic.

'I knew it, I knew it! She's so lovely isn't she? Wow. You're going out with Lily Hildebrand.'

'Ssh, you don't need to shout about it.'

'You're not going to be able to keep it a secret, you know.' She grins.

'Oh, god, I hadn't thought of that,' I say, pretending to be worried. So what if people talk about us? I don't care! 'You can tell Mum and Dad,' I say, because really that's one thing I'd rather not face just now. I've only ever had one official girlfriend before. They'll be so *interested*, and want to offer all sorts of advice about *being careful* and all that crap.

Just thinking about it makes me leave for sailing half an hour early to get out of the house. Or maybe it's because I'm so keen to see Lily again.

I decide that the kids are doing so well they don't need my complete attention. I take out the Mirror so

Lily can come with us, and I give her a bit of instruction as well as the youngsters.

The sun is shining so afterwards we go and buy ice creams and sit on the bench at the harbour, watching the fishing boats come in.

Everything is good.

Unfortunately this peace and harmony doesn't last long. The following morning Lily comes over to my house, but all she wants to talk about is the gala. She doesn't think Alice Beaumont is taking the wall painting seriously enough, and wants to know how many entries there are for the talent show. Because Gemma and I have entered she now thinks we're the best people to liaise with Kelly. She's willing to give advice if necessary. Gee, thanks.

And then she gets on to the raft race.

'We've got five definite entries,' she says happily, as she follows me out into the garden, 'and two or three possibles. It's going to be amazing!'

'Have you cleared it with John yet?' Although I know she's put out some of Sarah's posters, I haven't heard it mentioned recently. I'd kind of hoped it had died a death. I really wish I'd found a way to close Lily down on this idea, but so far I haven't.

'I'm sure John will be fine, as long as it doesn't interfere with his regatta races. Don't look so worried. It's going to be epic.'

I remember something Kelly mentioned when

Gemma and I were talking to her about the talent show. About the gala schedule. 'It's going to be, er, really difficult to have the raft race.'

'Listen, it's all organised—'

'There's been some mess-up with the guest of honour for the awards ceremony and the Gala Dance. He can't make it on the Saturday, so they've moved both to the Sunday. The awards are going to start at six, immediately after the last regatta race. They're already stressing about people being late for the awards, plus the noise of the races interfering, because the marquee is on Harbour Green. There's no way you can tack the raft race on to the end. They'll have a fit.'

Lily's expression darkens. I wait for an explosion. Then she just tosses her hair back and shrugs. 'Too bad for them. I can't cancel it now. And it's not like I want to go to the awards personally. It's always the same people up for Best Float, and hardly anyone even dances at the so-called "dance" afterwards. Let's just say those who want to stay for the raft race can stay, and those who don't can go.'

'But …' Why can't she just give in gracefully? 'The point is it will interfere completely. A raft race isn't going to be quiet, is it?'

'I don't see a problem. They'll be out on the water.'

'Listen, Lily. The main marquee is right on the waterfront, on the Harbour Green. If they see a whole lot of rafts setting up there they'll have the police on to you.'

'The Harbour Green is a ridiculous place for the marquee. I told them they should use the Town Square.'

'Which is currently a car park, so they can't. Can't you just cancel the raft race this year?'

She looks mutinous. 'Out of the question. I'm even entering a raft myself. I've got a really brilliant idea, but you don't have to get involved.'

'Good. Because I'm definitely *not* getting involved. I'll be busy doing the starting and finishing of most of the bloody regatta races. Sunday's the main day.'

'Well, you can do that and I'll do the raft race. It'll be fine. I'll ask Gemma to be my crew. Well, no, not Gemma. I'm sure I'll find someone who's up for it.'

I sigh. No matter what I say, she'll still push on with whatever it is she wants to do.

She's nodding reassuringly, as if all she needs to do is make *me* see sense. 'It'll be fine. Really. The rafts will only be around for half an hour or so, it's not as if the route is particularly long – from the bridge down to the sailing club and back. Why should anyone object to that?'

'What about all the setting up and packing away at the end? John Forsyth is bound to see you before you even get started, and he'll go ballistic.'

'He can't stop us,' she says, defiant now.

I throw my hands in the air, wondering if there is any possible way to make her change her mind. I just know this is going to be a disaster. And because it's on the water, I feel kind of responsible.

I try for another ten minutes or so, but there's nothing I can say that will sway her.

Later I try to get Gemma to talk to Lily, but she just shrugs and says it's pointless to argue. Then she wants to know how Lily and I are getting on now we're official – as though I want to talk about that! It's bad enough with Sarah asking questions.

Sometimes I just wish I was back to my old life, taking a back seat and not getting involved in *anything*. But only sometimes.

Lily

I'm really disappointed about Tom's attitude to the raft race. So what if we make a bit of noise and Simon Archer and John Forsyth aren't pleased? The aim of the gala is to involve people and have fun. This is just part of all that. A really good part, which fortunately, by the time they see it, will be too late to stop. But Tom clearly isn't going to come around, so I now need to find someone interested in building the raft I've thought up. I'm better on invention than construction, that's for sure. And I still haven't found a decent song to sing in the talent show. Gemma keeps coming up with really sappy ideas. I shoot those down in flames, but I haven't found anything better myself. It's pretty difficult to find something that a) I like and b) I can actually sing.

At the family meal a couple of evenings later (we have family meals every day now that Dad is home, and this time I cooked a not-quite-perfect risotto) I say, 'Either of you interested in helping me build a raft for the gala raft race? Or helping me choose something to perform at the Newton St Cuthbert's Talent Show?' I don't think my parents will be keen to be involved in either of these, but it's a topic of conversation and those aren't always easy to find.

'You're going to sing a song?' says Mum, sounding unflatteringly surprised.

'Well, it's either that or play a piano solo, and I really don't think I'm good enough.'

I wait for her to say something like she doesn't think so either, but fortunately Dad is more interested in my other question. He puts down his fork, giving up on the overcooked rice.

'You're building a raft? I didn't know there was going to be a raft race.'

'There is,' I say firmly. Don't they even look at the posters that I've put up? 'I'm planning to use milk cartons as the main flotation device. The plastic ones. I've been collecting them since I had the idea and so has Gemma. We've got ten already.'

'Ten won't be nearly enough,' says Dad, narrowing his eyes. 'You'll need at least a hundred, I would say. How many people are going to be on this raft?'

'Two. That's the minimum you're allowed. I'm sure we won't need that many cartons. We just need a base that floats and then maybe a chipboard platform or something on top.'

'No, Lily, that isn't going to work.'

I glare at him, annoyed. Why does everyone have to belittle my ideas? Then it occurs to me that he isn't just being critical, he's thinking it through. He looks interested. Wow. Even if he isn't here to build the thing (he's due to fly to Madrid in a couple of days' time) I can pick his brains beforehand. His initial training was in engineering afterall.

'We need to get the right ratio of floatation to cargo. I'll look into it after we've eaten. What are the rules? Are there any restrictions on design?'

'No, not really. It has to be handmade and all parts taken away at the end of the race.' I hadn't thought to put in any other rules. In fact, I'd only thought of the first one; the latter had come from Sarah who has goody-goody environmental tendencies.

Dad rubs his hands together. 'Let's see what we can come up with, shall we?'

'As long as it's safe,' says Mum. She's frowning, like she's trying hard to concentrate. I wonder what the drugs are doing to her. She listens to our conversations, but I'm not always sure she's following them.

I smile brightly. 'It'll be fine. We'll all wear life jackets, or *buoyancy aids* as they're called, and we can swim. And it's not like we'll be miles from the shore.'

'And the sailing club rescue boat will be there, won't it?' says Dad.

I nod, although I don't have a clue if it will or not. It'll be there for the regatta races so it should be okay.

After the meal Dad draws a really cool and far too

detailed plan of a raft. It incorporates some of my ideas (the empty milk containers) and a whole load of his (larger plastic containers).

'That looks brilliant,' I say. I'm impressed, but also worried. 'Where will I get all the stuff from? And how am I going to build it?'

'You can start collecting things now. There should be some empty diesel containers in the shed. You can get your friends to help assemble it all.'

'Possibly.' Gemma might help put it together, even if there's no way she'll go on it. And maybe I can involve Donny, who's taken to popping around occasionally to talk about the parade. I'm certainly not going to ask Tom. I realise I haven't actually said anything to Mum and Dad about Tom. They know I see quite a bit of him, but don't seem to think there's any particular reason for it. I'm glad. I don't like people interfering in my life. Their vague sympathy after stupid Jamie Abernethy broke up with me was bad enough.

Dad is so taken with the idea of the raft that he actually starts gathering bits and pieces together himself the next morning. Or it might be that he's bored senseless hanging around the house, but either way it's useful.

Dad has the radio blaring out classic rock (his taste is *awful*), and bits of wood and packing cases spread out all over the lawn. Then he remembers he's taking Mum out to lunch and leaves me to it. I look at Dad's plan, and slot a few bits of wood into the spaces where they seem to fit. It all seems pretty straightforward so I take it apart again and start to clear up. As I haul the final planks of wood inside the shed, I realise I've left the radio on and Aerosmith is playing. I'm starting to think this song is pretty chauvinistic, but it still makes me smile. I message Corinne the lyric *Everything about you is so F-I-N-E fine.* She replies with = *Famished, Impatient, Nonstop, Exhausted,* so I tell her to take a break and eat something. Another song comes on that catches my attention for a different reason. It's all about someone who "won't back down". That's something I can identify with. And the guy's voice isn't that great. If he can sing the song, surely I can too?

Inspired, I head up to my bedroom and search for the song online. It's easy to find because (surprise) it's called 'I Won't Back Down'. It's by some guy I've never heard of, but I don't need to have heard of him, I just need the words and the music. I check the lyrics and they're perfect. I've found the song for me!

I text Gemma and tell her I need her help. I would have liked to ask Tom to come round, too. But he's being so annoying about the raft race, and he's bound to recognise the implication of my chosen song's title and start going on at me again, so I don't bother contacting him.

Gemma is more than happy to sort out backing music for me and listen to me whining out the words over and over again.

'It's so you,' she says happily. She doesn't comment on the quality of the performance, but that doesn't matter. I'm not in it to win, am I? I agreed to take part and so I will.

Tom

It's the day of the first regatta race for the kids. Well, the evening, really, as we've scheduled things to kick off at six so working parents can come along and watch. Monday is the eleven-and-unders section. There are only seven kids in it, but they're pretty good, and excited about having an official race course set just for them.

The route goes up towards the harbour, so that anyone hanging around there can watch if they're interested. For once the tides are in our favour, and even the wind is okay, neither too strong nor too weak.

I haven't seen Lily much today because she's been at the park 'helping' with the wall painting. I feel sorry for Miss Barbour, the art teacher, but she should really have known better than to let Lily drag her into this. I went to take a look earlier and the results so far are ... *bright*.

Now Lily and I are sitting on the jetty, holding hands, watching the competitors get ready for the start. We're both avoiding any mention of her ridiculous raft race. That way we get on fine.

'Shouldn't you be out there helping?' she says. Well, we would get on fine if she wasn't always making useful suggestions.

'John's in his element doing this, and he's got two of his cronies in the rescue boat. I'm doing enough on Sunday for the main races. They haven't asked me to do anything today and I'm certainly not offering.'

Lily looks around, as though she'd like to find something else for me to do. Or for us to do – she isn't lazy. I say quickly, 'Look, we organised this whole thing, I've taught them for weeks, we even helped rig the boats earlier on. You've been painting all afternoon. Can't we just sit here and watch?'

'Okay,' she says, but she doesn't sound convinced. Her bottom lip is starting to stick out like it does when she feels she's being crossed. So I lean in and kiss her, just because I can. She has a really amazing mouth. Even when she's sulking, I want to kiss it. You never can tell with Lily, but this time she seems happy enough to be distracted. We only turn our attention back to the race when the final boat has finished and the youngsters are coming ashore again, high with the novelty of it all.

Some of them snigger when they see Lily and me together, but she ignores that with her usual aplomb and I hold my nerve and ignore them too. When I get home, quite a bit later, I find Sarah and Mum in the middle of a shouting match.

'I'm so much better! Why can't I go?'

'You don't want to overdo things, Sarah.'

'You're always going on at me to try things, now you don't want me to!'

'It's not that I don't want you to–'

'Stop fussing! I want to go out and do things like normal teenagers do.'

I would have liked to head straight upstairs and not get involved, but the door to the lounge is open and once they've seen me there's no escape.

'Er, everything okay?' I say, staying in the doorway to maximise the chances of a quick getaway.

'I want to go and watch the kids' races with you tomorrow. Mum won't let me.'

'I didn't say I wouldn't let you. Maybe if you went for half an hour. I could drive you down and you could sit in the car.'

'I don't want to sit in the car! I want to hang out with everyone else. I'm so sick of you making a performance out of every little thing.'

That is really unfair. Mum and Dad have been brilliant with Sarah, trying to let her set her own pace, trying to make her see when she's being totally unrealistic. Like she is now. Sometimes she refuses to try to do anything, but this time even I can see she wants to do too much. After the last time, which ended up in a dash to hospital, it isn't surprising Mum is so cautious.

I don't say any of this. Both of them are looking to me like each expects me to take their side. 'Where's Dad?' I ask.

'It's his bowls night,' says Mum. 'We'll talk about this in the morning, Sarah. All right?' She picks up their empty mugs and heads for the kitchen.

'I'm going. I don't care what they say.' Sarah looks mutinous, her eyes angry behind the glasses.

I say brightly, 'What've you been doing today?'

'What do you think? The usual. Homeschooling stuff, a walk to the park with Gemma, lying on my bed. God, my life is thrilling.'

'You don't need to do homeschooling. It's the holidays.'

'What else am I supposed to do? I'm so bored even modern studies was better than nothing.'

'I never did modern studies. Not my kind of thing.' Which she knows, but I'm trying to move the conversation on to easier territory.

'It's okay, I think I might prefer media studies, but I haven't got the coursework for that yet.'

There's a silence while we listen to Mum banging things around.

I say, 'I think I might head off to bed.'

'I think I'll come too. Before *she* starts up again.' She swings her feet to the floor and stands up, and I realise that I don't feel the need to help her. A few weeks ago it was a major effort for her to get up the stairs. Now she can do it without a second thought.

When we get to the top she says quietly, 'Are you worried about tomorrow?'

'What? Oh, results.' It might sound odd, but I'd forgotten tomorrow is the day we get our exam results. I've had a lot on my mind.

'Of course, you'll do really well,' she says.

'Hmm.' I wish she hadn't mentioned it. It means I'm awake on and off through the night, wondering if I completely messed up the physics paper. And the English one. And I'm not that confident about the others ...

My results arrive and I've got all my predicted grades. Mum and Dad are delighted, but I'm mostly relieved. One less thing to worry about. Gemma comes over to moan that the only subject she got an A in is music. I'm not sure why this is a problem, she didn't fail anything and it's music she wants to specialise in, but apparently it makes her a complete loser.

'How did Lily do?' I ask to distract her.

'Oh, don't you know? Pretty well. As in English, drama and media studies. And she didn't fail maths either, which she says is a miracle.'

At that moment I get a message from Lily saying just about the same thing. I think the three of us have done fine. Certainly well enough not to have to think about school stuff for a few more weeks.

My results have put Mum and Dad in such a good mood they agree a compromise with Sarah. She won't go to see the regatta race today, but if she's still feeling well and still keen, she can go in with me tomorrow. That's the day the various pipe bands are performing on Harbour Green after the races are over, so if she doesn't tire too quickly we'll stay and watch them, too.

She's so excited about this outing she spends most of Wednesday getting ready for it. Her eyes glow. She's wearing her hair loose and a bit of make-up. It's good to see her so happy.

Dad lets me drive the car when he takes Sarah, Gemma and me into town. We go by a circuitous route, so I can get more practice. After not liking it much at first, I now think it might be quite fun to be able to drive – properly, without supervision.

'You're so good,' says Gemma, disgusted. 'How did you get so good so quickly?'

'Because I have weekly lessons, and I practise. You're going to need to start properly, you know.'

I can see her in the mirror, scrunching her gingery eyebrows together and scowling. 'I'll never be this good.'

We spend the evening with Lily (who isn't nearly so complimentary about my driving, and far more jealous) and Donny who's started hanging out with us. Lily hisses to me, 'Don't mention exam results to Donny. He aced drama but didn't do so well otherwise.

His parents had a fit when Karl didn't do well last year so he's keeping a low profile.'

I take the hint and steer the conversation elsewhere. Not that I wanted to talk about results. The girls seem to be more into that. Sarah says practically nothing for the first half-hour, just listening and looking around, but gradually she begins to relax.

It's the under-fifteens race today. Because the weather's so warm there are plenty of people out watching, buying ice creams and hot dogs from the stalls by the harbour, generally having a good time. Lily is beaming around, like this is all her doing.

'Do you think we can go somewhere with a bit more shade?' asks Gemma after a while. She's wearing an enormous straw hat but we head for the Harbour Green, where there are a few trees.

'I don't worry about the sun,' says Donny, shaking off some of his gloom and holding out his very skinny brown arms. 'I tan really easily.'

'You're so lucky,' says Lily, although she's looking pretty brown (pretty and brown?) herself.

'You are,' says Sarah to Donny. And then, with great daring, 'And your hair is amazing. It's so golden and shiny.' Sarah's hair, like mine, is a wishy-washy dark blonde.

'Tell you a secret,' Donny winks, 'it's not natural.'

Sarah blushes because he's talking to her like she's one of the crowd.

'I couldn't be bothered with any of that,' says

Gemma, but Sarah looks interested. I wonder what she's planning now. I don't think Mum'll be too chuffed if she dyes her hair purple or something. Or maybe she will be, if it's a sign Sarah's finally getting better. But we've thought that so many times, and it has never happened. I'm not going to count on it happening now.

Sarah is in fact a bit pale and droopy by the end of the evening, but not nearly as bad as I'd feared. I remind myself it's normal to get tired. It's been a scorching day and even people who are fully fit are flagging, so it's probably just the weather. She makes me promise not to say anything to Mum and Dad. She's loved being out so much and is now determined to go to the dreaded (for me) talent show on Friday. We manage to get her into the house and up to her bedroom with minimum chat, so Mum and Dad only see her pleasure and not her lack of energy. If she has Thursday at home, and most of Friday, she should be okay.

Lily

I'd lost track of how preparations were going for the St Cuthbert's Talent Show, having been excluded from the committee and all that. Kelly seems to have taken to the whole organising thing, which is good of course, but I'd quite like to be able to check she's got everything covered. We don't want a disaster on our hands.

I wonder if Simon Archer is regretting not having me around. I would have done a bloody good job. Ah well, it'll be interesting to see how it pans out on the night. The rest of Gala Week is going pretty well, although I personally feel that if it hadn't been for the daily wall painting, and the sailing regatta running every evening, events would have been a bit on the thin side.

The talent show is to take place in the Town Hall, which has awful acoustics and not nearly enough seating. I'd suggested they use the main hall at school, which would have worked so much better, but they seemed to think using it during the holidays was too complicated. Their loss.

Now it's Friday and I realise I really haven't practised my song enough. I ask Gemma to come over in the afternoon to help, but she says she and Tom doing a final run-through of their own songs.

'I still haven't heard you play,' I say, peeved.

'I invited you the other day but you were busy with Donny.'

'He wanted to go over all the plans for the parade tomorrow. You know, timing is everything.' Plus Donny has agreed to do the raft race with me, so I have to keep on his good side.

'Yes, well. You could come over and listen to us now, if you want?'

'No, I really need to practise my own thing.' I don't tell her I haven't even learnt all the words yet.

'Then I suppose I'll see you at the Town Hall later.'

'Yes, fine, no problem,' I say airily. I won't even be able to get in a bit of private time with Tom, because he'll be with Gemma. It's annoying, but I'll just have to get on with it.

All I need to do is memorise the words. And sing them more or less in tune. So far the chorus is the only thing I'm absolutely sure of. "I won't back down" isn't a refrain I'm likely to forget!

As I'm going through it for about the fiftieth time, Mum appears at the door of my room. 'What on earth are you doing?'

It doesn't sound like she's impressed.

'Practising for the talent show. It's tonight.'

I think she'll go away then, but she doesn't. Instead she comes into the room and sits on the bed, not even commenting on its unmade state. 'Do you mind if I listen? I can prompt you, if you want. Have you got the words handy?'

I'm so stunned by this offer I hand over the sheet without a protest.

'Okay, here we go.' I tap start on my tablet.

On this attempt I get almost to the end before I mix up the words. Pity it isn't karaoke, where they have the words scrolling across the screen in front of you.

'I know this song,' says Mum. 'I haven't heard it for years, but it really suits your voice. Go on, have another try.'

Saying it suits my voice isn't necessarily a compliment, but it does mean my mother is interested in something I'm doing. I don't want to lose that feeling, so I do a couple more practices, just to keep her there. Then I suggest she comes along in the evening to watch. She looks doubtful. Since Dad went away it's been harder to get her to go out, and Corinne has only managed one short visit. But after a pause, she agrees. Even if she's only there for a short time, it'll be something. I don't think she's been along to watch me in anything for years, even when I had the lead in *The Crucible*. It feels good that she's coming. It feels like I'm doing something useful for her. I think, I really think, she might be getting better.

Tom

The Town Hall is absolutely packed for the talent show. Perhaps the committee should have taken up Lily's suggestion and held it in the school hall. I didn't expect the turnout to be this good and I don't think Simon Archer and Mrs Hebden did either. Initially entries were so low they thought they might have to cancel it. That's supposedly the whole reason I'm here.

Mrs Hebden is rushing round, flushed and irritable, trying to find more chairs and worrying that by bringing them in she's contravening fire regulations or something. For the first time since I'd agreed to play the guitar, I'm glad I'm a competitor. At least she can't drag me and Gemma into helping.

I see her eyeing Sarah and say quickly, 'Sarah needs to sit down. I think Gemma's mum was saving her a seat. In you go, Sarah.' Sarah shoots me an annoyed look, like she'd wanted to be asked to help. She'll learn!

Gemma and I head for the backstage area.

'I really don't think this is a good idea,' she says for at least the tenth time in the last half hour. 'I hate singing in public. Why did I agree to do this?'

It's no good telling her I would love to just drop out too. We can't, because everyone is expecting us to perform. Lily even seems to think Gemma has a chance of winning, and that this will somehow miraculously cure her lack of confidence. I don't have such high hopes but I'm not going to let her back out now.

'Come on. At least we're third on, we won't have too long to wait.'

We head into the room set aside for performers and Gemma stops so suddenly I crash into the back of her.

'Oh no!'

'What is it now?' I'm really losing patience.

'Jamie Abernethy is here. I didn't think he would be back. I can't sing in front of *him*.'

'You won't be in front of him,' I say. 'If he's in this room he must be a competitor, so he'll be at the back here while we're on stage.'

'But still …'

'For godsake, Gemma, get a grip!'

In honour of the performance Gemma has allowed her mother to put her hair up in a bun and apply some make-up. She's now gone so pale she looks yellow under the lights. She really needs to get over this Jamie Abernethy thing.

Fortunately Lily comes striding over. She's gone for the rock chick look: black jeans, black sleeveless

T-shirt, bandana around her head. She looks good, and not the slightest bit nervous herself. 'So you're here at last! I thought for a moment you'd backed out, despite needing all afternoon to yourselves to practise.'

I glare at her and say in a low voice, 'Gemma's panicking. Apparently having Jamie Abernethy around makes everything worse.'

'Oh, is he here?' Lily scans the room, frowning. Then she turns back to study her friend, who's swaying slightly as though she'd like to run out of the room but can't remember where the door is.

'Hey, Gem! Your hair looks great. Come over here and I'll touch up your make-up ...' I let her lead us over to one side, relieved to have her take charge.

Gemma tells Lily to leave her make-up well alone, and then slumps in silence on to a bench. I really hope Jamie is performing before us. The sooner he's out of the room the better.

Lily has moved on to moaning about the way they've organised the evening. 'There are too many acts to have the main session and then the final session all in one evening. I'd planned to run over two nights. I don't know why Kelly changed it.'

'There weren't many entries to begin with.'

'And now there are plenty. She should have been more flexible. Honestly.'

I scrutinise Lily, waiting for some sign she's chatting to hide interest in Jamie. He's looking very tanned, talking about his trip and attracting even more attention than usual. Apart from making sure she knows where he is so she can block Gemma's view of him, she seems to take no notice. Why should she? I'm her boyfriend now.

Lily

I wish I could go front of stage to see Gemma and Tom perform. Gemma is so nervous I thought for a while there she was going to be sick. And it seems that Tom was right about her having a thing about Jamie. Him being there is definitely making her more nervous. But I know that once she starts she'll be fine. We just need to make sure we get her on the stage to start.

I walk with them into the wings, but am stopped from going further by Mrs Hebden.

'Next contestants only, please.'

She sounds more harassed than bossy so I smile in a friendly way and say, 'Just keeping Gemma company.' I keep a tight hold of Gemma's arm, in case she makes a dash for it at this late stage, and only release it when Tom takes over to usher her on.

'Good luck,' I hiss, and am rewarded by a brief, bright smile. He isn't much less nervous than she is.

'I hope she doesn't freeze,' I say to Mrs Hebden, forgetting she and I aren't on the best of terms. 'If this goes right it will do her so much good.'

Mrs Hebden nods her agreement and we stand there, holding our breath, as the contestants' names and the song are announced. Tom begins the first chord.

I was right! As soon as Gemma starts singing, any tremor in her voice disappears. She's doing Burns's 'A Red, Red Rose', and doing it fantastically. Her voice soars and lilts, she hardly needs the support of the guitar.

Afterwards the applause is resounding. 'The best yet,' Mrs Hebden whispers to me. And then, when the two reappear, returns to her pompous mode. 'Off you go. Stay in the competitors' room, now, please. Lily, you'll be called when it's your turn.'

'You were amazing,' I say to Gemma, dancing around in my excitement. 'Really really good.'

'She was, wasn't she?' says Tom. 'Didn't need me there at all.'

'I did, I did. I'm so glad that's over. I hope we don't get through to the next round.'

Tom meets my eyes. There is no way she won't get through. 'I'd go and work on your second piece, if I were you,' I say. 'Just in case. Is it my turn now? Oh well, better get it over with.'

My performance is even more excruciating than I'd expected. Singing with attitude in your bedroom is so much easier than singing on stage. I even have the teeniest bit of sympathy for Gemma. Unsurprisingly, the applause I get is polite at best. Mum is there, sitting at the very end of one row, and she claps enthusiastically which is nice.

Tom is grinning when I get back into the competitors' room. 'Great song,' he says. 'We could hear it from here.' He doesn't comment on the actual singing, which is sensible. Gemma is all positive but I know she's only being kind.

The only act I'd really like to be able to watch, apart from Gemma, is Donny's. He's teamed up with a girl I recognise from one of the shops in town. Their clothes alone are enough to attract attention. Donny is wearing a miniskirt and the girl a three-piece suit.

'What are you singing?' I ask as they're hustled out.

'Lucky Stars.'

I look round at Tom and Gemma but they look blank too. The door of the contestants' room has been left open and we can hear as the music starts up. I realise I do recognise it. It's a duet where the couple are asking each other questions, first about being angry and then about love. But I don't think it's the singing that's getting the attention. The laughter starts low and then gets louder and louder.

I know we're not supposed to go out front but I don't care. I need to see this.

And it's worth seeing. They're singing a duet, but Donny is singing the boy's part while dressed like a girl, and the girl is singing the girl's part while dressed in the suit. And they're hamming up the actions like anything. Donny is a great character actor. He's down on one knee (showing way too much skinny thigh) like he's proposing. Mrs Hebden looks like she's about to have a heart attack when they get to a bit about being "sleepy" but they just go back to the chorus. What was she expecting, that they'd throw off their clothes or something? She hurries them off stage.

'Friends of yours?' says Jamie, having come out to watch too.

'Yes.' I give him my best glare.

'Heard about you wanting to get the gay crowd more involved. Is there something you're trying to tell us?'

'Get lost, Jamie.'

'Hey, sorry, it was just a joke. I think it's a great idea.' He smiles but I don't smile back.

I head over to where Tom and Gemma are practising. The rest of the evening passes quickly. There's an interval, with tea and sandwiches for the competitors, and then the four acts going through to the final round are announced. I don't make it, and nor does Donny (clearly this wasn't an audience vote!). Gemma and Tom are there, as I'd expected, along with screechy Kelly Smith, and an adult I don't know. And Jamie bloody Abernethy. It's *just* like him to come straight from the airport and schmooze the judges so well he gets through to the final.

'Those four acts are to remain here,' orders Mrs Hebden. 'Everyone else can go out front and listen. There aren't any seats, but you can stand along the walls. And hurry up. We're not supposed to be running this late.'

I manage not to say anything about how they wouldn't be running late if I'd been in charge of things.

The acts are called in a random order and by good luck or bad, Gemma is first. The song she's chosen this time is another Scots classic, 'Gloomy Winter's Noo Awa'. She sings beautifully as ever, but it's not the best song for this kind of competition. As the title suggests, it is gloomy, and doesn't fit the light summer evening. Still, she gets strong applause and I hope for the best. The judges are out of my line of sight, so I can't see how they react.

The other acts are okay, nothing special. And then comes Jamie.

'As some of you know, I've been away from Scotland for the last few weeks. I'm going to sing a song that really started to mean something to me during that time.' Ah, how heart-warming. The audience lap it up.

He launches into the unofficial anthem of homesick Scots, 'Caledonia'. I can tell he's won even before he starts the second verse. He sings well enough, although without Gemma's crystal clear notes. But he has the audience in his hands. They love this song, and they love him.

I'm right. Mrs Hebden brings all the four acts back on stage and the results are announced in reverse order. Gemma and Tom come second, but Jamie's won.

I try to remember that it's the taking part, not the winning, that counts, but I can't help feeling peeved. It would have meant so much more to Gemma if she'd won.

Gemma, of course, doesn't think so. She and Tom join us as I share my disappointment with Sarah.

'You two were the best,' I say, hugging them.

'You definitely were,' agrees Sarah, glowing with pride. 'You should have won.'

'Thank goodness we didn't.' Gemma shudders. 'I hadn't even realised the winner had to give a speech. Ugh! Imagine.'

'Tom could have done that,' I say, thinking how much better he would have been than Jamie gushing and thanking everyone. 'And you would have been fifty pounds better off.'

That's when I remember Mum. I'm useless. I'm so used to her not being around that it's easy to forget her when she is. Gemma's mother sees me looking at where Mum was sitting and says quietly, 'Your mum had to head home.'

'Oh.' I should be pleased she came at all. And I am. But I can't help noticing how Jamie's parents are all over him, and Gemma's parents are both here for the whole evening too.

'You did well, Lily,' says Gemma's dad now. 'Your song was … different. It made a nice change.'

'I thought you were really good,' says Sarah loyally.

I shrug. They're just being nice. And the important thing is that Gemma's confidence has been boosted, and Newton St Cuthbert's first talent show has been a definite success. Who would have thought it?

Oh that's right: *ME*.

Tom

The Gala Parade is due to start at two o'clock on the
Saturday afternoon. Sally-Anne is our spy and she's
been great at keeping us up-to-date with any changes.
I thought initially she might be a bit put out by Lily's
ideas, as they're bound to take attention away from
her. Instead she's become steadily more supportive,
even coming up with suggestions for the best place for
the Rainbow Court to congregate.

For maximum impact, it's been agreed that they'll
join the parade just as it turns on to the main street,
slipping in between the pipe band that leads it and
the float carrying the Gala Queen and her attendants.
It's going to cause chaos. Donny and Lily and Sally-
Anne don't care and I find I'm carried along by their
enthusiasm. I'm looking forward to this. I get Dad to
take Sarah and me into town and drop us off on the
main street. I choose what I think will be a good spot,
and we wait.

There are already quite a few people out, chatting, eating ice cream, starting to line the street in expectation. It's not like it's a massive parade, Newton St Cuthbert has never stretched to that, but there's the pipe band, the Gala Queen, three or four other floats, and the little children in their fancy dress. I think a lot of the spectators are friends and relatives of the fancy dress kids.

'I used to love the fancy dress parade,' sighs Sarah. 'Do you remember that fairy outfit Mum did for me? I loved that outfit.'

'And wore it until it fell to pieces.'

She smiles reminiscently. Just recently we've been having these conversations, recalling normal memories about normal brother and sister stuff, not about her being ill, not about her frustrations. I pat her shoulder. I don't want to make a big thing of it but I so much want this to be the way things are going to be from now on.

We hear the pipe band as it starts up and begins to get closer.

'They'll be here soon,' I say. I feel nervous now. For Lily, I think.

Then they round the corner and there they are in front of us. Lily is running alongside, taking photos. And oh my god someone has organised TV cameras to be here! Or maybe they come every year? I don't know, but they're certainly focussing on Donny and his friends today, who have slotted perfectly into the parade. There are those who came to the beach barbecue, and a few more as well. Some are dressed up to fit the court theme, and almost all have some kind of rainbow-coloured item on them – a hat, a scarf, even a wig. Donny's capering around everyone in his jesters' suit. He yells, 'Now, come on everyone, the dance! Everyone in time!' and he slides effortlessly in at the front and begins to do the steps.

The crowd have been watching, stunned. Now a few of them begin to clap. Donny gives them a wave but carries on with his steps. By now he's about the only one who's doing them right and the TV camera has gone in for a close-up. A man in drag waves the sign *Anyone Can Be a Queen!*

Sally-Anne gets up from her velvet throne and waves to the newcomers, before curtseying graciously. Good for her. The atmosphere has gone from vaguely jolly to surprised and excited. This is going well. Then I see a group of people coming from the other direction. Simon Archer and his cronies had been waiting on the temporary stage where Sally-Anne is to be crowned. Now they're storming down the street towards us, pushing their way through the pipe band, who get all out of step, and stopping in front of Donny's contingent.

'What is this? You can't be here!' Simon Archer is breathless and red in the face from running. 'This is a gala parade!'

Mrs Hebden is running up and down between the gatecrashers and the spectators, like she's big enough to be a one-person barrier. 'This isn't part of the programme,' she says loudly.

Sarah is holding on to me she's laughing so much. 'This is so brilliant. Did you see the man wearing the rainbow crown doing a cartwheel? It must be glued to his head.'

Simon Archer has come to a standstill close to us and is staring at the man with the crown, open-mouthed. It's not someone I know, but clearly Simon recognises him. The man sees him staring and hesitates.

Lily's shouting, 'Keep moving, everybody keep moving.' And quiet Jo, of all people, is the one who grabs the man with the crown and hustles him back into position.

I have to give the leader of the pipe band credit. Despite most of the gala committee pushing through his musicians, he carries right on marching. And because the band continues, Donny's group can follow on, and then it's Sally-Anne and the rest of the floats. Everyone claps these floats much harder than they have done in previous years and by the time the little ones have appeared in their fancy dress the whole town feels like one big party.

I can hear people around me: 'That was amazing!' 'I wouldn't have thought they'd allow it.' 'We've all got to move with the times.'

Simon Archer has stayed close to us, and I can see he's heard that last comment too. The TV camera swivels around and the presenter sticks a microphone in his face, 'Mr Archer, can you give us your views on the success of the new-look parade?'

'I … I …' He gulps and looks around desperately. 'It's lovely to see the little ones having fun … Must get back to the podium. We're crowning the queen …'

The presenter speaks to the camera herself. 'And as you can see, there is a great turnout here for the annual Gala Parade. It's safe to say this year's queen will hold the most inclusive court in Newton St Cuthbert's history …'

Simon Archer blanches, but it doesn't matter anymore. He might not be happy, but practically everyone else is. The town loves the new addition to the parade. Lily and Donny got their way.

Later, when we've walked up to where the queen is being crowned, I see Donny being interviewed by the TV presenter. She says, 'You seem to be one of the leaders here. Can you tell us what you hoped to achieve?'

It's the opening Donny needs.

'We wanted to show that the gala should be for everyone. We wanted everyone to feel included.'

The reporter says, 'And they didn't previously?'

He shakes his head. 'Previously the gala's always been about fancy dress for the kids and crowning the Gala Queen – a female Gala Queen carefully chosen by the same people every year. That's not exactly inclusive, is it? Or gender equal. So we thought about having a Gala King, and then about everyone who would still be excluded. Then, well, it just snowballed.'

The reporter is smiling as people come up to pat Donny on the back and tell him well done. 'You certainly took people by surprise. Were you nervous?'

'Maybe a little. But it was worth it. Look how happy everyone is.' He stops as a particularly hearty congratulation knocks his hat off.

'And speaking of fancy dress,' the reporter laughs, 'did you enjoy dressing up too? It looked like you were having a ball!'

Donny nods, but answers more seriously. 'We were using a fun method to get across an important message: that everyone should be free to be who they are. Not just during Gala Week, but all the time; and not just in big cities, but in small towns too.' Finally he winks, 'I mean, where better to harbour open minds than a seaside town like this one – right, Karen?'

Karen titters girlishly. 'Oh ferry funny!'

Donny grins in delight. This is completely his kind of thing. 'Don't anchorage me. You have no crew what you're getting into.

'Shore I do.'

'I'm *sea*rious. Schooner or later you'll regret it.'

Oh buoy ...

The cameraman struggles to keep his face straight, never mind his camera, as the interview descends into increasingly nautical – make that *naughty*cal – puns.

Yes, today has definitely brought a new angle to the Newton St Cuthbert Gala.

Lily

After the enormous success of the Gala Parade, I thought Tom would see sense about the raft race. But he doesn't. He won't back down about it interfering with the marquee and not having been cleared with John Forsyth. He even says it's probably not safe. I don't tell him there's no way I can stop the whole thing now. I just tell him to go and be the starter for the regatta races, or whatever it is he's doing. I don't need his help.

Gemma knows I'm pissed off and tries to make excuses for him.

'Look, I'm not bothered, okay? I'll manage on my own until Donny gets here.' I wish he'd hurry up, but I've learnt that timekeeping isn't one of his strong points.

'I'll help you,' Gemma offers.

I stare at her and she adds quickly, 'Just putting the raft together. I'm not actually going on it.'

'You know, one of these days you're going to have to deal with this ridiculous fear of water.' Normally I just accept that's the way Gemma is, but today I'm feeling impatient with the world. Okay, she nearly drowned when she was six or seven, but that was ages ago.

'I can swim,' she says stiffly. This is true. The new pool opened in Newton St Cuthbert soon after we'd started school. As soon as Gemma could do the obligatory one length, she gave up. I've never seen her in the water since.

'Yes, but– Oh, never mind. If you could help me carry everything down to the harbour, that would be great.'

I'm getting a bit worried about exactly where we're going to erect the rafts. It had seemed straightforward when I planned it in my head. The big patch of grass down towards the bridge is usually empty and there's a little slipway nearby where we can launch. The problem is half the grassy strip is taken up by the stupid marquee Tom was going on about. And as it's the ideal place for viewing the finishing line of the regatta races, the other half is packed with spectators. It's great that people are so interested but where are all the rafters going to congregate?

I finally decide that we'll just have to go to the far side of the bridge. It isn't so convenient, but it does have the advantage of keeping us out of sight of Simon, John and anyone else who might interfere, for a little longer. Not that I care what they think, of course, but I don't want a shouting match to spoil things now.

In the end, there are only four entries. I'm a bit disappointed, but hopefully if it's a success this year it'll grow in the future. The girl from the sailing club is there with her brother and another group, and there are four older men who've come out from Dumfries with a very professional-looking raft, clearly determined to win. Which reminds me, I haven't actually done anything about a prize yet ... Ah well, something will probably occur to me.

It takes Gemma and me nearly an hour to carry the various bits of the raft from the house down to the waterside. Sarah turns out to be a godsend. She's come to watch the afternoon regatta races and when she sees us carrying the last pieces of plywood and floats, she follows on behind. 'You're entering the raft race? Wow, that's amazing!' I'm not sure if she means the fact that I'm entering, or the raft itself.

'My dad designed it. It's all supposed to kind of clip together ...' I frown down at it, hoping for enlightenment. I really wish Dad was home to help.

'I think maybe you've got it the wrong way round.' This is Sarah. She's also frowning, but in the manner of one studying a jigsaw puzzle with a view to actually assembling it. 'Yes, look, this bit goes here. And maybe you need to turn that round. Yeah, that fits.'

She's right. I've only seen the thing erected once, on the lawn at home, and clearly hadn't paid enough attention. But now it takes shape again and fifteen minutes before the planned start it's all clipped together and we're ready to go. We've even managed to get it down the muddy bank and into the water.

The only problem is, Donny still hasn't appeared.

'I'll go and check out the Harbour Green,' says Gemma. 'See if he's looking for us there.'

'Thanks.'

'What will you do if he doesn't turn up?' asks Sarah. 'There are supposed to be two people on board, aren't there?'

I pull a face. I'm not going to back out now. 'I'll go on my own if I have to. It's not as though I'm likely to win so it won't really matter.' I don't really fancy being out on this flimsy contraption alone, but I'm not going to admit that.

The tide isn't great, either. It's coming in, which was fine for the sailing boats, but now it's almost at its highest and will turn soon. I've no idea how that will affect the race. I wish I'd paid more attention to Tom's explanations of wind and tide, but it's too late now. I could try and question Sarah, she also knows a bit about sailing, but she's chewing her lip and frowning so I decide not to.

'No sign of Donny,' said Gemma, returning. 'He's not very reliable, is he?'

'He did well with the parade.'

'Aye. That was pretty amazing, wasn't it?'

We grin at each other, then I remember I've got a

raft to board. 'Can you hold this rope while I get on?' I try to ignore all the comments and strange looks from the other entrants. Okay, I'm the youngest person here and the raft does look a bit odd, but the whole idea is to encourage variety, isn't it?

The other rafts are much more solid than Dad's clever (I hope) design. They've used massive oil cans and polystyrene floats and lots of rope. Obviously they need to be heftier if they're going to take the weight of three or four men, but I'm starting to wish mine didn't look quite so fragile.

It's now one minute to five and still no sign of Donny. I check my phone and realise there's a message from him. *Sorry, can't make it. Parents just seen my Higher results. Can't get away right now.*

Shit! That's just what I need. From the sound of cheering, the last regatta race has finished on the far side of the bridge and there's nothing to keep us from heading off. I need to make a decision.

'Everyone good to go?' I shout. People nod and wave. 'You know the course? Down to the sailing club and back. Here, Alice, you can do the countdown and blow the whistle to start us.'

Alice Beaumont is one of the few spectators who have followed us to this side of the bridge. The rest are on the harbour green watching the end of the sailing races. I toss Alice the whistle and reposition myself on the raft.

'Pass me the oar,' I say to Gemma, indicating the

makeshift paddle that Dad has made from a spade I had as a child.

'You can't go on your own,' she says, frantically chewing the ends of her hair. 'Do you want – do you want me to go with you?'

I'm impressed by the offer, but there's no way I'm taking her up on it. A rickety home-made raft is not the best way to introduce her to life on the water.

'You're a star for offering, but really I'll be fine.'

Sarah jumps up, like she's come to a decision. 'I'm going to come with you.' She kicks off her shoes and pulls on the spare life jacket.

'Sarah, I don't think it's a good idea ...'

'You need someone. It'll be fun.' Before I can stop her she's clambered aboard, the second oar (a covered tennis racket) in one hand. 'Wow, this is – Aargh!'

The raft wobbles wildly and almost tips both of us in, but we scramble towards the centre and save ourselves.

'On your marks!' shouts Alice Beaumont. 'Three, two, one.' And she blows the whistle loud and long.

Sarah starts paddling madly and I give up the argument. It's too late to get her back on shore, and if I don't concentrate and start paddling myself we'll both end up in the water. The splashes hitting my bare arms are shockingly cold, reminding me just how bad it would be if Sarah fell in.

'Okay, calm down,' I say, raising my voice so she can hear me above the shouts of the men. 'Not so frantic. We don't want to capsize.'

'Come on, paddle! We're ahead. The barrel raft is going round in circles and one of the other men has fallen in already!'

'Concentrate,' I snap, concerned by how much she's jigging around. True, someone is already in the river, but he's a healthy man, he isn't going to catch his death.

His friends drag him back on board and we head under the bridge.

There's still quite a crowd on the Harbour Green who turn as we appear and began to laugh and clap. Excellent! That's what this is all about.

The crew from Dumfries are already pulling ahead, paddling in unison. The others are larking around and providing great entertainment. I just concentrate on keeping my deathtrap afloat.

Mostly you can't make out individual voices, amidst the shouts from the shore and the splashing of the makeshift oars, but there's one I know only too well. 'What on earth is going on? Who organised this ridiculous event?' That's Simon Archer, and easy to ignore.

The next voice is even less welcome. 'Sarah!' It's Tom. 'Sarah, what the f– What the hell are you doing? Bring that thing ashore right now!'

'Ignore him,' hisses Sarah. 'They're always trying to stop me doing things. This is so much fun!' She throws back her head and laughs. She looks really pretty when she's happy. I'm pleased she's enjoying it, but mostly I'm just concentrating on keeping the raft going in more or less a straight line and not listing too much to either side. It's harder the farther downriver we go. The rush of the tide meeting the flow of the river creates a turbulence I hadn't expected. I'm really not sure Dad's raft is up to this, especially when I see the debris that the tide has brought in.

'Look, we're nearly at the sailing club, why don't we turn back now?' I say breathlessly. There's a fish crate floating near us. If we hit that we'll definitely go over.

'No way! We've got to go around the red buoy, that's the course we agreed.'

'But …' Even the men's rafts, strung firmly together with the ropes, look too unstable for the waves we're now encountering. The problem is if Sarah won't do as I ask, it's safer to keep paddling with her.

'Okay … Maybe … Look, stay near the centre of this thing, please. I don't like the way the floats at the edges are shifting about.'

I have a vague recollection of Dad saying that when we assembled the raft we had to make sure the larger floats were on the outside. I squint down. It really doesn't look like that's what we've done. Which means we haven't put it together according to the plans. Which means …

My heart sinks at the realisation that we're not just on a flimsy raft, but on an incorrectly assembled flimsy raft. Sarah gives a crow of delight, 'Here's the buoy! And we're second. Round we go …'

Turning direction is the final straw. The bits of wood we'd so cleverly slotted together come apart, the floats bob up and the whole raft begins to disintegrate.

'Uh-oooh,' says Sarah, giggling. It feels like slow motion as the structure breaks into pieces, some of which fly up out of the water. I try to grab Sarah, but she topples over with an enormous splash and I follow, head first.

I struggle to right myself. 'Ugh. Sarah? Sarah!' I doggy-paddle round in a circle, batting away bits of raft blocking my view. She was here a few seconds ago, she can swim, she has a life jacket on …

Then I see her, floating among the wreckage, right next to the fish crate I saw earlier. There's blood over one eye. She isn't moving.

'SARAH!'

I swim towards her, hampered by my clothes and more stupid bits of wood and plastic. I try to remember my life-saving lessons from years ago. Make sure the victim's head is above water, make sure they're breathing. I catch hold of her, kicking hard against the tide. At least the buoyancy aid is doing its job and her face is clear of the water. She's breathing. I'm almost certain.

A shout comes from the men's raft. 'Hang on, we're almost with you.' They've seen what happened and turned back. They push the debris away and draw up alongside us. 'Hold her steady, lass, you're doing fine. The rescue boat will be with us in a minute.'

I try to say there won't be a rescue boat, because I haven't arranged one. Then I turn to the sound of an outboard motor. Planned or not, the rescue boat with John Forsyth at the helm is almost upon us.

I hold on to the men's raft with one hand and Sarah with the other. I have never in my life been so relieved to see anything as that boat. Even if it does have Tom on board, looking white with fury.

Tom

I know Lily never listens to anyone, but this is beyond crazy. She's actually gone ahead with the raft race. Well, so what, if she wants to kill herself that's her business. But to take Sarah on the raft with her? Sarah who hasn't been out on the water for years, who was only allowed to come down this afternoon because she promised to sit and watch and not do anything too taxing?

I'd intended to keep an eye on her but lost track because I was manning the start/finish line for the official races. The next thing I know she's out there, on the water, on what looks like the contents of a plastic recycling bin. I start running along the shore, shouting, and then see John Forsyth is launching the rescue boat again and jump in.

When I see the raft break up I feel like I'm going to be sick. Thank god we were already heading towards them. But even before we get there, I can see something is wrong. Lily is swimming, the men are shouting, but where the hell is Sarah? And then I see her, lying completely still in the water at Lily's side.

She's unconscious when we drag her out. I want to head straight for the shore, leave Lily where she is, but John won't do that. With the help of the men he hoists her into the boat as well. I'm only interested in Sarah. She's a sickly white, with blood oozing from a cut over one eye. I turn her on her side. Has she swallowed much water?

She stirs as I bump her against the fibre glass side of the boat. 'Err … What happened?' She spits out some seawater, but not much, and tries to sit up.

'Stay where you are,' I say.

'Bit of an accident,' says Lily, taking Sarah's hand and chaffing it, although she's shivering so much herself she can hardly control her movements. 'Sorry about that.'

I don't know if she's talking to Sarah or me but I ignore her.

When we reach the jetty we're met by the paramedics from St John's Ambulance, and they whisk Sarah away.

I'll never trust Lily Hildebrand again. Never. She's a self-obsessed fool. She could have killed Sarah. Even now we've no idea what the repercussions of this might be. The ambulance crew have stripped off her wet clothes and wrapped her in blankets. I wait silently as they check her pulse and temperature and all that stuff. Mum and Dad have joined us in the First Aid tent, looking as stunned as I feel.

'She seems remarkably fine,' says one of the paramedics. 'A bit shocked, of course, and she'll have a nasty bruise over one eye, but no long-term damage done.'

'I am fine,' says Sarah through chattering teeth. They've given her a hot drink to sip and she has trouble holding it, her hands are shaking so much.

'You're freezing,' I say.

'N-not really. It's just sh-shock.'

'Why were you out there?' says Mum. 'I don't understand.'

'I was with L-Lily. Donny was supposed to crew for her but he let her down. Is Lily all right? She fell in too.'

'She'll be fine,' I say. I have no idea where she is but have no doubt she'll be okay. The Lily Hildebrands of this world always fall on their feet. Why wasn't she the one knocked unconscious? That would have been much more fitting.

Apparently she's being cared for in the next cubicle. A few minutes later she shuffles through, also wrapped in a blanket, her normally wild hair wet and lank and her cheeks pale.

'How's Sarah? I'm so sorry.'

'I'm sure it wasn't your fault,' says Dad doubtfully.

'No, it w-wasn't,' says Sarah. 'I got on the raft myself. I didn't give her any choice.'

Lily shrugs, looking unfamiliarly lost. She's watching me.

'If Sarah gets ill again,' I say, 'I will *never* forgive you.'

Lily

Gemma's mum Barbara takes me home. Gemma wants to come too but I say no.

I want a hot bath and the chance to get over the fright I've had. When I saw Sarah so pale and motionless, her face bleeding ... She seems fine now, no worse than I am, but I don't blame Tom for what he said. Even if it doesn't have any long-term effects on Sarah, it could have done. It could have killed her.

Mum looks confused when we arrive, but Barbara explains what happened and Mum manages to be concerned. She tells me to have a bath and then go straight to bed. She even brings me up a tray with soup and bread and butter, like she used to do when I was ill as a kid. She's frowning, like this is really hard for her, but at least she's doing it.

'I'm sorry I didn't manage to come watch,' she says. 'I just felt too tired.'

'That's okay,' I say. It wouldn't have made any difference.

'I'm sorry,' she says again. 'Maybe one day we can do something together, just the two of us? That would be good, wouldn't it?'

'That would be nice.'

The phone rings and I say, 'I don't want to talk to anyone.' It's likely to be John Forsyth, wanting to rant at me; or Sarah's parents, suddenly realising how much danger I'd put their daughter in.

Mum lets it go to answerphone. 'Turn off your mobile, too,' she says. 'Tonight you just need a break from it all.'

She's right. I turn off my phone and lie down with the shutters closed so that the room is almost dark. I think I can hear the faint strains of music from the marquee where the Gala Dance is taking place. It takes me ages to fall asleep, but it isn't because of that. I should have listened to Tom. Why do I always think I know best? I can't get Sarah's white, lifeless face out of my mind.

The next day I feel a bit better. Donny comes by to apologise for missing the race, and Gemma to see how I am. She gives me the latest on Sarah, who is being kept in bed but apparently doing okay. I don't ask her how Tom is and she doesn't say.

The day after that Mum and I do actually go out together. She decides a walk in the Galloway Forest is just what we need. It is a lovely place. And it's nice being there just the two of us, nobody asking questions or criticising. Mum can be a very calming presence.

Later Dad comes home and he wants to hear all about everything. He's very disappointed that his design failed so spectacularly. I have to explain it was probably because we'd put it together wrong, but he's still put out.

'Maybe I'll go and see if there are any bits left over, see if I can work out what happened. I've already thought of some improvements for next year.'

I just sigh and say nothing. Like there's going to be a *next year*.

Surprisingly, I don't get any hassle from Simon Archer or John Forsyth. I decide this is because they think I've suffered enough.

Sarah messages me to see if I'm okay and insists she is absolutely fine. She doesn't answer when I ask if she's been allowed to get up yet, though. It's good to know she's all right, but I'd far rather hear from Tom. He stays silent.

The following day Dad comes out to find me when I'm lying on the sunlounger on the deck. I'm not so much trying to top-up my tan as keep away from everyone. Half the time I feel close to tears, which is so not like me. I need to get a hold of myself.

'You're a good girl, Lily,' he says, à propos of nothing.

'What?' I squint up at him.

'All the things you've done for the gala and the town. And you've really helped your mum over the last few weeks.'

I sit up cautiously. Even confused, I know sudden movements on a sunlounger can be disastrous. 'I haven't done much.' I wait for what he's really come to tell me. He must be softening me up for something.

'You have. Your mum is doing much better.'

'That's because she's taking her medicine, like you said.'

'Maybe. But she really appreciates the effort you've made to do more of the cooking. And I do, too, of course. You've been a big help. It can't have been easy, the last few months.'

'Er. Thanks.' I'm surprised he's noticed. Apart from Corinne, no one in the family has really seemed to think that what's been going on could have had an impact on me.

Suddenly the hurt and worry I've been feeling and not acknowledging for months comes bubbling up. I'm fed up of all this not saying things. I'm worried Dad is going to pretend everything is normal and fine when it's *not*. I'm not going to let him just push everything under the carpet. 'Dad, you do know Mum isn't completely well, don't you? We're helping, it's great that you've been home so much more, and Corinne too, but … but you can't pretend that she hasn't been ill. That she isn't *still* ill.'

He looks surprised by my tone, but then nods slowly. 'I am aware of that, Lily. These things take time.' He clears his throat and goes back to what I presume he wanted to talk about. 'Anyway, having the roof replaced and a new coat of paint on the outside has made me remember why I've always loved this house. It looks great.'

'I'm certainly glad to see the back of the scaffolding.'

I'm still waiting. Are we selling the house? Is something else going on? I wish he'd just get on with it.

'I've been thinking about all the other things we could do. Smarten up the conservatory, maybe redecorate the drawing room. If I'm going to be home more I think we need to freshen the place up.'

'*Are* you going to be home more?'

He frowns, like my interruptions aren't part of the script.

'I am. We live in a wonderful place, and yet I'm hardly home. I don't see nearly enough of you, or your mother. And, er, as you say, your mother needs me. I probably shouldn't have been away so much in the last few years.'

Wow, that's quite an admission, coming from Dad.

He continues, 'This is probably the last year you're going to be living at home, so I'm rethinking my work life. I'm going to revamp the study to be a proper home office and make this my base. I'll rent out the London flat.'

'You're moving back home?'

'I never moved out,' he says, a bit testily. 'But I am going to be home more. It makes sense financially, and this way I'll be around for your last year of school. Then if you head off to uni, I'll be here for your mum.'

'Oh,' I say. 'Well, that's great.' I'm not convinced I actually want him home more on my own account (what if he starts interfering?) but on the whole this is good news. It looks like I've sort of got my family back. I wonder what Mum will make of having him around. Knowing Dad, when he's not conference calling around the world, he'll be networking with the local bigwigs, and taking charge of the golf club again. Still, everyone to their own.

He nods to me and strides back into the house. I can almost hear him thinking, *That's one more thing ticked off, what's next on the list?*

I lie down again. I'm pleased by this development, I really am. And relieved not to be moving any time soon. But it isn't long before I'm back to thinking about Tom. Missing Tom.

And there's absolutely nothing I can do. No point in getting in touch again. Nothing I can say in my defence, no way of making him less pissed off with me. I'm pretty pissed off with myself. People warned me a raft race could be dangerous but I'd just gone ahead anyway, so sure that nothing bad would happen. I was an idiot. And although it appears nothing awful has happened to Sarah, the whole fiasco has cost me any chance I might have had of a proper relationship with Tom.

I miss him like a physical ache. Miss his snorts of laughter, his disagreeing with me, his kisses and his touch. So what if he is stubborn and won't always go along with my plans? I really like him like that. Only now it's too late.

Tom

Sarah keeps going on at me about getting in touch with Lily. After the first day I'm not so blindly furious, but I still can't understand how she could do something so stupid. Courting unpopularity by upsetting the gala committee is one thing; putting Sarah at risk like that is unforgiveable.

'But I'm fine, there've been no ill effects,' my sister insists. It's three days after the accident, and she's been saying this pretty much all day and every day since. It's not completely true, though. She hasn't come down with pneumonia, or even a cold. The cut is healing and she claims the headache cleared after the first day. But she's back to being tired, even though she tries to hide it. Back to lying on her bed or the settee most of the day. Back to pretending she's reading a book so it seems like she's doing something, when she's not even turning the pages.

Part of me knows that I could have done more to avoid this. I shouldn't have left her alone at the regatta, especially anywhere near Lily. I knew Lily hadn't given up on the raft idea. I should have known there was a risk if Sarah was hanging around with her.

Sarah doesn't seem to see it this way. 'For goodness sake, I can look after myself,' she says that evening. I'm perched on the end of her bed and she pushes herself into a sitting position so she can glare at me. 'I may be a bit tired, but I'm not ill. And who knows, maybe I'm tired because I was out so much last week, not because of falling in the water. Stop acting like it's the end of the world! If you don't go and see Lily soon, I'm going to ask her to come here. You're being ridiculous.'

'Fine. Ask her. I'm not stopping you.' It's not like Lily can do any more damage, is it?

'If you're so annoyed with her, why don't you just break up with her?'

I leave the room.

It takes me another couple of days to realise that maybe Sarah is right, and that I do want to see Lily again. I need to see her again. The anger has worn off, and I miss her.

I don't know how I feel about us anymore, but I suppose there's only one way to find out.

I send a message on Friday morning: *Do you want to come sailing? I'm taking Dad's Mirror out.*

She replies after half an hour: *Are you sure you're brave enough to go out on the water with me?*

I smile. *I think I can handle it. Meet you at the clubhouse in an hour?*

I arrive first and start rigging the Mirror. Lily doesn't approach with quite her normal swagger, but nor is she hesitant. She's tied her dark hair in a jaunty ponytail and dressed in shorts and a sleeveless T-shirt. After a couple of days of rain it's back to being sunny.

'Hi there,' she says, standing at a little distance with her hands on her hips. It's like she's standing back because she expects me to start shouting or something.

'Can you get the centreboard?' I say politely. 'Otherwise we're just about ready.'

She does that, then pulls on her wet shoes and a buoyancy aid and waits for further instruction. She's being so compliant that I narrow my eyes at her, suspecting she's overdoing it to be difficult, but she doesn't meet my eyes. She isn't acting, she's genuinely ill at ease.

The tide is high so we only need to drag the boat-trolley to the jetty and launch from there. The wind is brisker than I'd expected and I let the mainsail out a little and push the tiller away so we head out to the open sea.

'Where do you want to go?'

Lily has settled in her usual place at the front, holding the sheet for the jib. 'I don't mind. You decide.'

Now she's making me edgy! I know we'll have to talk at some point, but I'd kind of thought we'd get back to our old easy relationship while we were busy.

Either that isn't what she wants, or she's more upset than I'd realised.

'We'll go up towards Borra and then we'll see,' I say. She nods.

It's an easy sail, the water's calm and the breeze strong but steady, a southerly which is pretty near perfect. It's cool against the skin but I'm glad I've put on sunglasses because the sun is blinding as it reflects off the water. In conditions like this there's no way I can't enjoy myself. I relax, enjoying the sounds of the waves and the sails, giving Lily only one or two hints as to how to adjust the jib. We should have gone out earlier and brought food with us so we could stay out all day.

Lily seems less tense, too. She looks about, tossing strands of hair from her eyes.

'It's been an amazing summer,' I say by way of conversation. 'I can't remember so much sunshine for years.'

'It's been pretty good,' she agrees.

We're now just out from the beach at Borra. It was here the boom hit her head, here we went ashore and first kissed. I keep on sailing, round the next headland to a wider beach called Sandhead. This is a place we haven't been together. No memories. Somewhere we can start anew.

Or not.

I turn the boat towards the shore. 'Come on, let's sit on the sand for a bit.'

We pull the dinghy out of the water and then walk up above the high tide line. We aren't touching, certainly not holding hands. It's all wrong.

It takes ages to reach dry sand. I'd forgotten how shallow the bay is here. Lily immediately drops down onto it and draws her knees up. She looks out at the silvery blue water and pale blue sky.

'I don't know what else I can say. I've said I'm sorry. I should have listened to you about the raft race. I should never have let Sarah out on the raft. I should have insisted we turn back once I realised how rough it was.'

I sit down beside her and breathe in carefully. 'Sarah can be hard to persuade when she has her heart set on something.'

'But still. If I hadn't started rowing too she would have had to give in. She couldn't race on her own.'

'But she could have upset the raft. Gemma said she was quite hyper.'

'Why are you being so understanding now?' She turns to face me for the first time, dark eyes narrowed against the sun.

'I'm just saying I can see how it happened.' I push my sunglasses up so I can see her better.

'And Sarah really is okay?' She shudders then, hunching her shoulders in. 'She says she is, but I keep thinking of how she looked before I could get hold of her, all white and blank ...'

For the first time I realise how awful it must have been for Lily, too. She's the one who took Sarah out on the raft, but she's also the one who rescued her. She held on to her until the other boats came.

I reach out slowly and take her hand. 'I'm sorry. It must have been horrible for you. But you didn't panic, you were great. John Forsyth said you did everything right. Apart from going out on the raft in the first place, of course.'

She gives a slight smile. 'Yes, that was just a teeny weeny mistake.'

'And it's over now. Probably no long-term effects.' I realise that Sarah's right. We can't know for sure what pulls her up and down. There's no point assuming it was the fall. She's been up and down before, and today she did seem a bit brighter.

Lily moves so that she's facing me. 'But what if there had been? What if someone had – had died?'

'They didn't. Aren't you always the one who says you can't not do things just because there's risk involved?'

'Yes, yes, but ...' She releases my hand so she can wave both of hers around, much more like the normal, animated Lily. 'But it's the first time I've really realised, you know, that things can go wrong. *Do* go wrong. And what if next time ... It was horrible, really horrible, seeing Sarah like that.'

I think of all the times I've wanted Lily to slow down, think first. Now I want her back to the way she was. The real Lily is hard work, but she's fascinating and exciting and definitely worth the effort.

'Hey, stop feeling so sorry for yourself. You'll learn from this, but you shouldn't stop doing the things you do. And people are responsible for themselves, too. That's what Sarah's been saying. It's not all up to you – or me – you know.' It's odd to find myself quoting Sarah.

'I suppose … But, god, Tom, it was so *awful*. I really thought …'

She looks at me with eyes wide, lips soft and quivering. What can I do but lean in and kiss her?

'Stop worrying,' I say. Then another kiss. 'It's going to be fine.' And another. 'You're fine.'

I don't know if it's her idea or mine, but soon we're lying on the warm sand and conversation is the last thing on our minds.

Lily

After a while I pull away. I scoot down slightly to put my head on his shoulder. Tom drapes his arm across my back.

'You know something, Lily Hildebrand?' he says against my loosened hair. 'I think I really like you.'

'Don't say it like it's a surprise!'

I feel him smile. 'It's not a surprise anymore. I just thought I'd tell you, that's all.'

'You know I'll still be irritating and bossy and do things people don't approve of, don't you? Even if I do understand it's a good idea to listen to advice. Sometimes.'

'So? I'll either do those things with you, or I won't. I can make up my own mind.'

I smile then too. 'Yes, you can.' I tilt my face up, kissing the soft skin where his neck and shoulder meet. He smells perfect, like sea and sand and Tom.

I say softly, 'You know something, Tom Owen?

I quite like you, too.'

His fingers stroke my arm in gentle circles, and his chest bounces with a little laugh, but we don't say any more. We don't need to.

It's peaceful and still. I'm not worrying about his family or mine. Not working to make things happen or stop them. Not trying to be Fantastic, Interesting, Noteworthy or Exceptional. Just being me.

And I really am fine.

Just fine.

ACKNOWLEDGEMENTS

Firstly, many thanks to my long-term writing buddies Pia Fenton, Claire Watts and Kate Thomson. I wouldn't be here without you. The Paisley Piranhas will always rule!

Immense gratitude to Imogen Howson for believing in *Lily*, and to Kate Nash of KNLA Ltd for being such a great, patient and sensible agent.

I'd also like to express my thanks to all at Sweet Cherry Publishing for turning a manuscript into a real book. You've been amazing.

Much appreciation to George Moorehead for being my sailing consultant (all mistakes are of course my own) and, along with Alex Stewart, Zack Stewart, Elspeth Nicholson, Marianne Nicholson and Livia Nicholson, for putting up with my endless questions about favourite music, slang, technology – and any other obscure point that occurred to me!

Big shout-out to the Romantic Novelists Association for making the life of a writer so much more fun than it would otherwise be.

And, finally, thanks to David, for being there.